MYSTERIES & MONSTERS

by

Ed Craft
&
Lisa E. Carmody

INFINITY
PUBLISHING.COM

Copyright © 2009 by Ed Craft & Lisa E. Carmody

All rights reserved. No part of this book shall be reproduced or transmitted in any form or by any means, electronic, mechanical, magnetic, photographic including photocopying, recording or by any information storage and retrieval system, without prior written permission of the publisher. No patent liability is assumed with respect to the use of the information contained herein. Although every precaution has been taken in the preparation of this book, the publisher and author assume no responsibility for errors or omissions. Neither is any liability assumed for damages resulting from the use of the information contained herein.

ISBN 0-7414-5428-9

Published by:

INFINITY
PUBLISHING.COM

1094 New DeHaven Street, Suite 100
West Conshohocken, PA 19428-2713
Info@buybooksontheweb.com
www.buybooksontheweb.com
Toll-free (877) BUY BOOK
Local Phone (610) 941-9999
Fax (610) 941-9959

Printed in the United States of America

Published May 2009

Table of Contents

Introduction 1
Alien Abductions 3
Area 51 7
Ark Of The Covenant 9
Atlantis 15
Alp 20
Ballygally Castle Hotel 22
Banshee 23
Beast Of Bray Road 25
Bermuda Triangle 28
Bible Code 29
Black Helicopters 31
Blood Countess 32
Castle Poenari 35
Cattle Mutilations 36
Champ 38
Chupacabra 39
Coral Castle 41
Crop Circles 43
Dead Sea Scrolls 46
Devil's School 47
Dragon's Triangle 48
Dybbuk 49
Easter Island 52

Eisenhower Meets ET 54
Electronic Voice Phenomena 55
Elementals 58
Extra Sensory Perception 60
Face On Mars 63
Faerie Circles 65
Fatima 66
Fountain Of Youth 67
Gandillon Werewolves 70
Giza Death Star 71
Giants In The Desert Of California 73
Golem Of Prague 73
Hampton Court Palace 75
Hell's Hum 76
Interstate 4 Death Zone 78
Jack The Ripper 81
Jersey Devil 83
Kennedy Assassination 86
Knights Templar 88
Kongomato 90
Leap Castle 93
Ley Lines 96
Mason Inn House 99
Mothman 101
Native Americans And Their Perspective On
    Ghosts/Spirits 104

Nuckelavee	106
Out Of Body Experiences	108
Pike Place Market	110
Queen Anne's (Boleyn) Ghost	113
Roanoke Island And The Lost Colony	116
Stone Of Destiny	119
Stonehenge	121
Table-Tipping	123
Tutankhamen's Curse	125
Uisneach	127
Unidentified Submersible Objects	128
Valentino's Ghost	131
Valley Of The Moon	132
Winchester Mystery House	134
Yeti	137

Introduction

From the first day that consciousness entered the minds of men and women, we have sought answers to everything around us. Since the dawn of humankind, there have always been strange and unexplained phenomena that we have sought explanations for, some of which have continued to elude investigators to this day. They range in variety from those of the darkest recesses of the human mind to those from the deep recesses of the Universe itself. With all of man's self acclaimed superiority over the laws of science, there are still questions that we are unable to answer such as the full potential and abilities of the human mind itself, the strange and frightening creatures that roam the Earth and the origins of humankind. Even questions as to whether or not we are alone on this rock as it spins through the darkness of time and space and if there is more to life after our bodies give way to the passage of time.

With the passage of each year, the list of the strange and unexplained grows as humans multiply and spread their seed further into the deepest and uninhabited parts of the planet and right out into the fringes of our solar system. As we grow and expand, so do the new mysteries that we discover and add to the list. This book is an attempt to delve into some of the strangest mysteries, monsters and unexplained phenomena that still seem to plaque the minds of humankind. The authors have attempted to present the material in a non-biased manner so as to allow the reader to examine the details of each case for himself or herself and do with the information as he or she sees fit. But be forewarned, that the evidence may not provide the answers that your soul is searching for.

Some of the mysteries mentioned in the book have existed since humans first learned to write. Yet others are the creations of or discoveries from the modern era. Either way, these cases still remain unsolved. Skeptics and debunkers strive to prove their cases as to who, what, where, when and why when it comes to these mysteries but proof beyond a reasonable doubt still avoids their tireless efforts, very much the same as it does for a prosecutor in an O.J. Simpson trial. Many philosophers, scientists, leaders, religious figures, investigators, researchers and average citizens have all sought answers to these questions at one point or another. The explanations for these mysteries vary greatly and are typically supported by the reader's own individual hypothesis, or beliefs.

A

Alien Abductions

Since the beginning of the twentieth century, millions of people worldwide have reported encountering strange lights and alien crafts just prior to being abducted by extraterrestrial entities. Once on board the strange alien crafts, the abductees are usually subjected to a variety of invasive medical experiments. It has been theorized that the reason for the abductions is to conduct genetic tests and engineering experiments on human beings.

Solar Physicist David Webb of Massachusetts has publicly stated that he estimates that one out of every eight individual witnesses to a UFO has been abducted by extraterrestrials. In 1982, The Massachusetts Institute of Technology held a conference and estimated that there are several hundred thousand to three million people in the United States that have had an abduction experience at least once. On some occasions the abductions may continue to reoccur over one individual's lifetime. But each and every time the abductee has little or no recollection of the events that occurred until much later or under regressive hypnosis.

Of all the UFO abduction cases that stand out among the rest, none can compare to the first publicly recorded case in history. There have been only three cases that stand out in the minds of the world as "proof positive" for the phenomena. They are the Travis Walton case, the Whitely Strieber case and the point of focus here, the Betty and Barney Hill case.

Without the information and courage brought forth by Betty and Barney Hill the world would have never known about the phenomena. The case of Betty and

Barney Hill stands out as the best example of the abduction phenomena, as it was the first to ever be noted in the mainstream. One of the factors that lend creditability to their testimony is the fact that Betty Hill was a Caucasian female and Barney Hill was a Black male during the time of their encounter. Both were very much in love and very much devoted to bringing equal rights to all people of the world. They were both very active in the social issues of the 1960's and very well liked and respected in their community. The last thing that they would do is to jeopardize their reputations, standing or causes within the community during the turbulent times of change involved with the 60's. The very last thing in the world they needed was to be labeled as "another UFO nut."

Their story and entry into the annals of the unexplained began on September 15, 1961 when Barney, a mailman on the New Hampshire Civil Rights Commission set up by the governor, decided to surprise his loving wife with a trip to Niagara Falls. Betty, a social worker and supervisor of the New Hampshire Welfare Department, was overwhelmed and very pleased to learn that she would be able to spend time away from their daily routine to share in their love and joy after being married 16 months earlier. The couple packed up their bags and the cash they had on hand as the banks were closed, and headed on their way. Seeming like the trip of a lifetime for two newlyweds, they ended their trip and began the return trip home on September 19, 1961. It was what happened on their trip home that made headlines and history around the world.

While on their way home from Niagara Falls, the couple noticed a bright light in the sky. The object first appeared as an unusually bright star that grew in intensity. They decided to stop and investigate. Using a pair of binoculars that Barney had placed in the car, he observed a "pancake" shaped object with windows. As

Barney observed the craft he noticed what appeared to be "people" inside starring back at him and, suddenly, like Alice looking through the looking glass, the couple's honeymoon was about to turn into a night that would haunt them to their graves. The events of that evening were so significant that they would be documented in the official U.S. Air Force's Project Blue Book report on unidentified objects.

As the Hills stood outside their car observing the object, Betty with the naked eye and Barney with his binoculars, the couple began to feel fear rising inside of them and decided to err on the side of caution, get back in their car and continue their trip home. When they arrived at home they were still in shock over the events of the night, but were left even more puzzled over the fact that they had lost two hours' time during their return trip that they could not account for. Being rational people they both acknowledged the event to each other and decided to chalk it up as a simple case of cerebral flatulence.

They would go on about their daily lives, but the "missing time" and a sense of darkness would continue to plaque them both. Finally in 1964, the true scope of the events of that evening three years earlier would come to the surface. While under hypnosis, the pair revealed the real terror of their unearthly encounter during their lost two hours.

The pair, under hypnosis, later described the full details of their encounter with the strange light while the Hills traveled south on Route 3 near Lincoln, New Hampshire. After spotting the light in the night sky the couple observed the object actually land on the road in front of them. The couple was powerless as their vehicle stopped working and the object began to open. During their hypnotic regression session, they recalled being taken from their car and taken on board a strange craft. Once inside the couple was taken to separate rooms where each were stripped naked and subjected to invasive medical tests. So traumatic were the experiments that Betty recalled the pain she felt as her abductors inserted a needle-like instrument into her abdomen. She said that her abductors were doing a pregnancy test of some type. Interestingly, the test that Betty described would come to resemble amniocentesis testing that human medicine would develop several years later.

While their abductors seemed to be using humans as lab rats, Betty would recall that their intentions were not to harm, but to test. She was able to recall a map that was shown to her by one of her abductors. It was a map of stars that indicated where they came from.

While debunkers scoffed at the Hill's story, investigators took it more seriously. It turns out that this case provided one piece of evidence that could not, and has not been explained to this day which was Betty's "star map." This piece of evidence first appeared to be made up, but as time passed and science grew, the significance of the map would become clear. Betty recalled that they beings told her that they were from Zeta Reticuli and also was able to remember the map that the beings showed her. What is shocking is that Betty had no knowledge or training in astronomy, yet her "star map" was later determined to be a valid depiction of an actual star system.

Another UFO abductee wrote a best selling book about his encounter with the unexplained. Whitley Strieber first told his story after being so troubled by it that it left him in a suicidal state. His horrifying and bizarre telling of an encounter with beings from outside of this planet brought a new meaning of terror to the abduction phenomena.

While running my own internet radio show, Magick Mind Radio, I had the privilege of airing on the same network and just prior to Strieber and what I gained from him was his true sense of concern that the phenomena he encountered does have an effect on us all. His fragmented recollections of his abduction and treatment still haunt him to this day, but he has chosen to use his experience to send the world a warning.

Countless others have come forward from Travis Walton to one of my former co-hosts, Heidi Hollis. They all range in socio-economic backgrounds and geographic locations, but their stories all seem to involve a strange group of extraterrestrials that have the ability to manipulate humans on many levels from the peaceful to the terrifying. Research has shown that there is clearly more than one type of phenomena occurring, but that at least one of them still remains potentially, "out of this world."

Area 51

Officially designated the "Nellis Air Force Bombing and Gunnery Range," the base did not officially exist until the 1990's when a group of family members from some former base employees filed a federal law suit against the government regarding the burning of toxic waste at the "nonexistent" base. After being forced to admit the existence of the base, the government was relieved of any responsibility for anything that may have, or could occur at the base under the guise of National Security and a special executive order issued by then President Bill Clinton protecting the base from any lawsuits.

With the controversy over the toxic materials being used and burned at the base put to rest under the executive order, the controversy over the goings-on at the base continue to this day. In 1989, a physicist by the name of Bob Lazar came forward claiming that he had worked at a secret area of the base he called Area

S-4. What Lazar described to the world was shocking at first, but would later become a battle cry for public seeking answers as to what is really going on at the base behind the curtain of "black projects."

Lazar made a claim that he was hired to work on a special project at the base to back engineer an alien space craft that had been recovered by the U.S. Government. He claimed that the craft he worked on was located in a series of nine hangars, each housing a different alien craft in various conditions of disrepair. Lazar claimed that he was not only shown the alien craft in their hangars, but that he was also taken to a room where he was left alone with a series of documents describing everything from the engines to the alien inhabitants themselves. Lazar's involvement at the base ended when he attempted to bring some friends to a remote location to observe a test flight of one of the craft. Unfortunately for Lazar, his story would be one that would be quickly discredited as his past history began to unravel. By the time the smoke began to clear on his story, Lazar had been discredited as a brothel running con man, but the rumors of alien space craft at the base would persist.

Things at the base settled down again until March of 1993 when an article in Popular Mechanics told of how a top secret spy plane had been under construction at the base, but that the base itself had closed down and relocated. The Popular Mechanics article was not surprising since both the B-52 and the SR-71 had been developed at the secret base. It was not a stretch that a Mach 6 aircraft was also being developed there. What was surprising is the articles claim that the base had been closed. Upon further inspection, it turned out that the base had not been closed and was very much open for business as usual.

Prior to Bob Lazar's claims linking Area 51 to alien space craft, there was Colonel Philip J. Corso, who was on General Douglas MacArthur's intelligence staff and later on President Dwight Eisenhower's Security Council. Corso turned out to be one of the most controversial key players in the UFO mystery. He claimed that he was given personal charge over recovered alien space craft that he distributed to various compartmentalized government agencies for study and research. He also claimed that the recovered alien technologies that he was in charge of distributing was used to reverse engineer such modern Earthly technologies as fiber optics, lasers, the transistor and many other high tech devices.

Combined with the secret projects at Area 51 and the claims by individuals like Lazar and Corso, the controversy over whether or not the government actually has recovered alien craft on the desert base in Nevada remains. The truth will probably never be known and instead remains under the catch-all label "A Matter of National Security."

Ark of the Covenant

The Ark of the Covenant is a vessel that was created by the Israelites that held the broken tablets that Moses received from God on Mount Sinai. The tablets contained the Ten Commandments that were broken by Moses upon his return from the mountain. It also contained the rod of Aaron and manna, the food that sustained the Israelites during their time wandering the desert. The Ark was considered to be the "earthly throne of God," and was eventually placed in the Tabernacle of the Temple of the Solomon. It is said to be the single most powerful object to have ever existed on Earth, possessing the very power of God.

Specific details for the construction of the Ark are provided in Exodus 25 in the Bible. It was made from acacia wood about two cubits and a half (about 3ft 9in) in length, a cubit and a half in height (about 2ft 3in) and a cubit and a half (about 2ft 3in) in width. It was overlaid with pure gold, both inside and outside with a molding of pure gold. There were four pure gold rings, one on each corner. Inside the rings were permanently placed two poles made of acacia wood that were also overlaid with pure gold. These poles were used to carry the Ark when it was not in its tabernacle. No one was permitted to touch the Ark itself and only a select few were permitted to carry it by the poles.

On top of the Ark was placed a cover made of pure gold that was known as the Mercy Seat. At each end of the Mercy Seat sat a cherub which was made from a single piece of gold. The cherubim faced each other and their wings were raised toward the Mercy Seat. It was from the Mercy Seat that God is said to have communicated with the priests. The Ark was carried by the Israelites during their years in the desert. It provided them with safety during that period and later would be used in battle with the enemies of the Israelites. One of the most famous biblical tales of its use involved the city of Jericho, whose walls crumbled after the Ark was carried in a procession around outside the city. Each time it completed a circle around the city the Israelites would blow their horns one time. Upon completion of the third circle the horns were blown one final time and the walls of Jericho came crashing down.

The legend of the Ark's power is recounted during a battle with the Philistines. The Israelites had been defeated by them in battle several times and decided to take the Ark with them on their final battle with the Philistines. The Israelites had hoped that the sight of the Ark would place the fear of God in their enemies. It did not and the battle was once again lost to the Philistines, who captured the Ark during the battle.

Feeling that their victory and capture of the Ark was a sign that their Gods were more powerful they proudly displayed the Ark as a symbol of that victory. It did not take long for things to begin to go wrong for the Philistines after their capture of the Ark. They quickly became victims of a mysterious plague and mice were always present wherever the Ark was placed.

During the time of the Philistine possession of the Ark, the mysterious plague may seem to be related to the Ark itself, but in reality the presence of the mice could account for rodent related disease. The fact that the mice were commonly present near the Ark could be attributed to the fact that it contained the manna, a potential food source that would attract mice and rats which carried disease. In this instance, the Ark of the Covenant could have been considered the first use of biological warfare. Bait the Ark with food, attract mice and infect a walled city with plague from the mice. While this is just conjecture, it is a plausible explanation for the mysterious plague. With their city blanketed in death, the Philistines placed the Ark on a cart and drove it out of their city. The Ark was eventually recovered again by the Israelites.

It was during the time of King David that the Ark would find its high place in the city of Jerusalem. During his reign as king, David declared the city of Jerusalem to be the capital of Israel. He had the Ark taken to the city and eventually placed in the Temple of Solomon were it stayed until the invasion of Israel by the Babylonian king Nebuchadnezzar II. After the battle the Babylonians were victorious and pillaged the city of Jerusalem, taking everything of value and keeping very detailed records of everything that was taken. When all was said and done, the Ark had disappeared forever. What makes the Ark's disappearance even stranger is that none of the meticulous records kept by the Babylonians contains any reference to the Ark of the

Covenant being recovered. What makes this strange is the fact that the Babylonian records of the items taken from Israel were so detailed that they recorded every single fork, cup, plate and other trivial items and treasures, but no record was ever taken of a treasure as great as the Ark. The Babylonians never once mentioned in their records anything about the most prized possession of the Israelites.

Theories about the Ark itself and its disappearance abound. One such theory about the Ark pertains to the power it possessed. One rumor speaks of the Ark having been recreated by scientists in modern times to test its powers. The rumors and stories state that the recreation was so high in radioactivity that it had to be immediately destroyed. Unfortunately, recreating an object of pure gold of that size would be so cost prohibitive that there is no financial way for anyone to obtain funding for such testing based on the median gold rate and the amount of gold it would take to build. Another factor preventing such a test is that the actual weight of the gold used in the original Ark's construction is not given. There is no way to know how much gold would be needed to recreate the Ark. While we do know that the Ark was overlaid with gold, we do not know how thick that overlay was. We also have no way of knowing if any details were deliberately left out of the Ark's construction when it was written down by the Israelites.

Some researchers have even speculated that the Ark was a communication device given to the Israelites by an extraterrestrial race that guided them through the desert. Others speculate that the Ark may have been some type of power generator that was similar to one that was once placed in the Great Pyramid. This theory is supported by its proponents in the fact that the Ark was built based on Moses' instructions. Since Moses was Egyptian, the connection has been made by some that he had the knowledge to build such a device based on teachings from the priests of ancient Egypt.

The speculation as to what the Ark actually was and what it actually did is as widespread as the hypothesis regarding its disappearance and possible location. The first was that it was actually destroyed during the Babylonian occupation of Israel. But the Talmud, the ancient history book of Israel, states that the Ark was actually taken away by the faithful just prior to the invasion by the Babylonians. The exact location as to where the Ark may have been taken is another mystery. Some speculate that it was taken back to Mount Sinai, the mountain of God, in Egypt where it was placed in a cave where it remains to this day.

Another possible location is the temple mound in Jerusalem. The city is built on top of numerous natural and man-made caves and tunnels. Since the concept of "holy place" is not confined to a specific spot, but to a specific space, it is suggested by some researchers that the Ark was never removed from the sacred space of the temple, but that it was simply moved to a location to a safe and holy space below the actual temple. Following the end of the Babylonian occupation of Israel, the temple was rebuilt on its original foundation, since it was a "holy place." When the temple was rebuilt the Ark was not placed back in it, but may have remained below where only a few knew of its location.

This theory was investigated back in the 1970's and 1980's by a group of Jewish rabbis who actually began to tunnel under the temple mound until they were eventually forced to stop their efforts due to the political implications of digging under what had become the most sacred place in the Islamic religion, the Dome of the Rock. At the time their efforts were stopped they had come to within yards of where they believed the Ark to still be resting below the temple mound. Efforts to try to continue their digging were permanently halted and the tunnel sealed in the interest of preserving peace between in that region.

One theory as to what happened to the Ark suggests that it is not lost at all, but actually still exists in a known location. According to this account, King Solomon's son stole the Ark. His son was the progeny of his union with the Queen of Sheba. It is claimed by the inhabitants of Aksum, Ethiopia, that Solomon's son brought the Ark to Ethiopia. A variation of this theory is that it was not stolen by Solomon's son, but was taken there by Hebrews that left Israel just prior the Babylonian occupation.

During the 16th century Muslims invaded Abyssinia, Ethiopia which had become predominately Christian during the spread of the religion throughout the Roman Empire around 300 CE. During their invasion, the Muslim forces left a wake of destruction. The destroyed many of the places and symbols of Christendom in Abyssinia, This included those on the small island of Tana Kirkos, which sits on the Lake Tana. The Ark is said to have been taken by Solomon's son and kept there ever since. After the Muslim invasion in the 16th century a modestly small cathedral was built to house the surviving Ark where it still remains today. The cathedral is maintained and guarded by a single monk that never leaves the cathedral. The structure is surrounded by a modest fence, through which can occasionally be seen the guardian monk taking in some fresh air. The monk will rarely speak to anyone, but when he does it is only from within the safety of the fence. He admittedly defends the fact that the Ark is actually in the tiny cathedral, but the Ark has never been seen by anyone but the monks that have guarded it.

The Ark has always been the object of desire by many. It has even been rumored that the Knights Templar actually discovered the Ark under the temple mound during their occupation of the Temple during the Crusades. It was during the occupation that the Knights Templar began to suddenly grow in wealth and power. Strange historical accounts state the Ark was brought back to France in 1128 by the Knights Templar where they purportedly unlocked the Ark's secrets, but to this day never revealed them.

Another mysterious twist in the tale of the Ark transpired in 2001 when a wooden tablet containing a representation of the Ark was found by Reverend John Mcluckie. The wooden tablet was found in a cupboard in Saint John's Episcopal Church in Edinburgh, Scotland. The tablet that represented the Ark of the Covenant was eventually turned over to the Ethiopian Orthodox Christians in 2002 after being recognized, by Mcluckie who had lived in Ethiopia, as belonging to them.

The search for the Ark of the Covenant continues as the faithful seek to protect its powers, and the powerful seek to exploit it. If the Ark has been found and does reside in the care of a select group of people, their reasons for keeping its existence secret may well be warranted.

Atlantis

The first written account of Atlantis comes from the Greek scholar Plato (428/7-348/7 B.C.E.) in his work known as the Socratic Dialogues. He described Atlantis as an island continent that was west of Greece, "beyond the Pillars of Hercules." The Pillars of Hercules has been interpreted in modern times to indicate the Strait of Gibraltar. Plato also told of the great technology and power of the Atlantean people. But even with all their great power and technology, they were eventually unable to prevent or stop a great natural disaster that sent their great city to the darkest depths of the ocean.

So powerful were the Atlanteans that they had a Navy that was able to establish colonies throughout Africa and Western Europe some 8,000 years prior to Plato's account of them. The name Atlantis is one that we now use in reference to this mystery. It is the name that was used in Plato's Greek description of the lost City State, but accounts of the land and its people can be found on nearly every continent. They vary by name, but the accounts of the Atlantean people and their tragedy remain the same. They were referred to as the Aalu by the ancient Egyptians, Ablach by the ancient Celts, Adapa by the ancient Babylonians, Abnakis by the North American Algonquian people, the Atali by the Native American Cherokee people and Atu by the ancient Sumerians.

If the story of Atlantis were based on the work of Plato alone, the existence of such a place would be in question. The Socratic Dialogues that mention Atlantis is actually a conglomerate work of fiction and fact in which the fictitious character in work is named after the actual Greek scholar, Socrates, a real person. Plato had intended the work to be an imagined conversation between both real and fictitious characters. It was not written as a historical account. The actual reference to the Atlantis is contained within the pages of the Conjoined Dialogues around 360 B.C.E. and was a part of the overall work known as the Socratic Dialogues.

What makes the existence of Atlantis a real possibility is a combination of Plato's account in combination with those of other civilizations, some more ancient that those of Plato, such as those by the Sumerians. All of accounts of the Atlanteans attest to the fact that they were a seafaring nation with wide spread influence, trade and wealth. Descriptions of the island itself tell of a veritable fortress by itself, interlaid with natural and man-made waterways that made it difficult to invade their city directly.

The capital city of Atlantis was supposed to be encircled by three canals that divided the land into three rings. The canals were filled with water from river in the mountains. A wall stood on each of the rings surrounding the inner city circle. Each wall was made from stone and was covered in a different metal, each more impressive than the last as they progressed inward. The outermost wall was completely covered in copper. The middle wall was covered in tin and the innermost wall with a vibrant and beautiful Orichalcum, which was a pink version of gold. The actual composition of this metal is not known and was said to be the creation of Atlantean alchemists. Support that the mysterious metal actually did exist came in 1916 when the British War Office in India obtained a small elephant shaped incense burner that was made from a similar strange and unidentified metal. The British eventually determined that the metal contained a mixture of nickel and gold.

In the center of the city proper, was supposed to have sat the Temple of Poseidon. References to the temple state that it was 600 foot long and 300 foot wide. According to Plato, the temple was "barbaric" in appearance. He also described it as having the exterior walls covered in gold with a blue tiled courtyard. Inside the courtyard sat a statue of each of Atlantis' kings and their wives. The interior of the courtyard was supposed to have a garden that was filled with plants and trees from all over the world. The interior of the temple was described by Plato to have been covered in ivory, gold, silver and the mysterious orchiduim, all of which were lost when the city was fell during the great disaster.

Modern interest in the lost city began in 1882, when Ignatius Donnelly wrote his controversial book, *Atlantis: The Andeluvian World*. In his book, he suggested that all ancient civilizations of the world were the result of the relocation of Atlanteans that had managed to survive the catastrophe the destroyed their home. Support for his theory came in the form of ancient monuments around the world that seemed to parallel those of the Atlanteans. Donnelly used the ancient pyramids of Egypt as one example. But he could have just as easily used examples such as the Temple of the Sun in Cuzco or the royal palace center in the excavated Sumerian city of Khorsabad.

Following Donnelly's book, a flood of speculation as to just how much technology that the Atlanteans possessed ensued. Stories and tales began to evolve that they had mastered flight and could generate electricity. Some individuals even began to claim that they had mastered nuclear technology. But the technological feats of the Atlanteans were not the only thing speculated about. One particular source of their power would also become the focus of many. It has been said that they possessed strange crystals that generated large amounts of energy and that the knowledge for using such crystals came from extraterrestrials. Extraterrestrials were supposedly responsible for interbreeding with humans to create the Atlantean people.

In the late 1960's the Atlantean tale would take on yet another facet as a strange road like structure was found under the water just off the coast of the Bimini Islands. The strange structure, now known as the "Bimini Wall," would have been written off as another oddity were it not for the predictions of Edgar Cayce (1877-1945), who predicted that a portion of the lost city would be found off the coast of Bimini during that time period.

Support for the actual existence of Atlantis may lay in its own destruction. We now know that during the period of between 12,000 and 10,000 B.C.E. Earth was experiencing the end of an ice age. With the warming of temperatures, came the melting of ice that increased the sea levels around the world. During this period of Earth change there were also many earthquakes, volcanic eruptions and climate changes that occurred. It is very possible, that the destruction of Atlantis occurred during this time period and could, though not probable, be verified through disasters that were recorded by other civilizations during that time. However, to this day no such record has ever been found.

With real support for the existence of Atlantis very shaky and speculative, new potential evidence was discovered in 2001, when investigators were exploring an area off of the coast of Cuba. Using a Remotely Operated Underwater Vehicle (ROV), they discovered what appeared to be man-made stone structures on the ocean floor. Photos of the structures were examined by representatives from Advanced Digital Communications, a Canadian based company. They were also examined by the Cuban Academy of Sciences. Both concluded that the structures shown at a depth of 2,100 feet appeared to be a man-made urban center. Their estimates as to the age of the structures were between 6,000 and 1,500 years prior to the Great Pyramid at Giza.

With the jury still out on the actual one time existence of Atlantis, potential candidates for its ruins continue to abound world wide. It is possible that given continued efforts by researchers and the growing level of technology available to search for the lost city, the truth will be uncovered and we can learn if Atlantis was an actual place or it is just be a conglomeration of tales from various cities lost to disasters. These tales could have been compiled into one single legend to remind future generations to heed the lessons of the past or face the consequences for their actions.

Alp

In 1679, the German theologian Phillip Rohr published a treatise titled *De Masticatione Mortnorum (On the Chewing Dead)*. His work became a seminal part of the vast amount of literature available on vampires. It discussed the beliefs of clergy and the devoted that the dead could return from the grave to bite and chew the living. The idea itself stemmed from the belief in a cannibalistic, blood-drinking race of little men.

The Alp would lay in wait and attack weary travelers that ventured down lonely and dark wooded roads. The Alp were the manifestation of the prevalent Germanic folklore that perpetuated the belief that the dead could come back to feed off of the living. Always violent and hostile, the Alp would often attack their living victims and devour them. Their legend became the European foundation for tales of vampires, werewolves and other flesh devouring creatures of the night.

As time passed and the tales of their horrors grew, these bloodthirsty dwarfs became associated with witchcraft and sorcery, taking on the ability to control and manipulate their victims with the powers of their mind. Unfortunately, there is little consistency in the tales of their horrors.

The Austrian version of the Alp was one that presented a particularly horrifying threat to its female victims. The Alp would focus its attack on women and young girls as they slept. Like a sexual predator, the Alp would molest its female victim like the incubi of ancient Rome. Always male, the Alp would focus its attack on the family and friends that they left behind in life. When a child was born it was closely inspected for marks that might indicate its future potential for becoming an Alp after death. When someone was suspected of being an Alp, the mother was always blamed as the cause. Sometimes it would be a berry that she ate during pregnancy that had been spat on by an Alp or if she had not behaved properly during her pregnancy. A tell-tale sign that a child would become an Alp was that they were born with a thin membrane across its face. While some societies looked at such a birth as a sign of good luck the German and Austrian societies took it as a sign that the newborn child would enter the ranks of the undead.

Primarily conceived as a part of German and Austrian folklore tales of the Alp, they are so ingrained in our own modern society that stories about their horrors are told to our children in the form of fairy tales such as Rumplestilskin or the child-eating witch in Hansel and Gretel. Their representations can even be found in modern times resting in gardens in the form of garden gnomes, whether chewing on the flesh of the living, inducing nightmares in sleeping victims or causing seizures. The terror of the Alp is one that lends credibility to the concept of learning to understand the world around us, rather than blame the dead for our troubles.

B

Ballygally Castle Hotel

A beautiful teal colored Scottish castle that overlooks the sea and located in Northern Ireland, it is a picturesque sight straight out of a postcard until the sun sets. With the moon in the background at night, the castle becomes a page out of a horror novel. Its small windows look out over the sea, but one window looks out from what the staff calls the "Ghost Room." The room is located in the corner turret of the castle on the North Channel side facing the Irish Sea. This room is one that nobody ever stays in, despite the fact that the Ballygally is a three-star hotel. The hotel was built onto the castle in the 1950's.

The castle was originally built by James Shaw, who came to the location from Northern Ireland in 1625. When he arrived, he took it upon himself to build the castle in its current location just 20 miles north of Belfast, Ireland where the French chateau-style castle still stands to this day. Seeking to make his home secure, he built it with stone walls that are five feet thick.

Shortly after completing the castle, Shaw took Lady Isobel Shaw for his bride in the hopes of producing a male heir. Within a year of their marriage, the Lady Shaw gave birth to their first child, but to James' displeasure, the child was a girl and not a male heir. The girl was the result of the Lady Shaw's adulterous affair with a sailor. So angry was James Shaw that he locked his young bride in the turret room of the castle. The story then becomes blurred, because it is not known for sure if the Lady Shaw leaped to her death from the turret or if James had her thrown from it.

Employees at the hotel have reported seeing a ghostly apparition and strange events in that Ghost Room located in the castle turret. But the ghostly activity in the castle is not limited to the turret Ghost Room. Visitors and employees of the castle hotel have reported strange occurrences in the four rooms located below the turret room. All four of the rooms are still used as part of the hotel and are available to visitors upon request.

Visitors that stay in the rooms below the Ghost Room are sometimes greeted in the night by the touch or sounds of a child laughing and playing. Other ghostly tales of the castle also abound. On one occasion, a group of businessmen were scheduled to stay in the hotel and were planning on having their dinner in the castle's dining room when they arrived. The room is known as the "Dungeon Room" and offers guests an elegant dining experience with its old world charm. The room was set up for dinner, prior to the guests' arrival and the staff went on about their business. That evening, when the doors opened, the guests and staff were met by a shambles of disarray. The drinking glasses had been placed in a circle on the table and the napkins had been scattered across the table. Whether or not one has a belief in ghosts, the events that take place at this castle seem to defy reason and logic.

Banshee

If you are descended from one of the five major Irish families such as the O'Neills, O'Briens, O'Connors, O'Gradys and Kavanaughs, then you may be familiar with the legend of an Irish female spirit who serves as a messenger to forewarn of an impending death. This supposedly happens even if the member of one of those families had died far away and news of his or her death had not yet come.

The term for this Irish messenger of death is best known by the anglicized version "banshee." According to several resources, the word banshee comes from these old Irish words, *bean sídhe or bean sí*. *Bean* means "woman and *sídhe* means "of the mounds" which is a common description of a fairy woman. The Scottish version is either *bean shìdh* or *bean shìdh*. Another type of the Scottish banshee is a *bean nighe*.

In any case, the banshees are believed to be the descendents of ancient Celtic deities, most specifically the triple aspects of the goddess of war and death, *Badhbh, Macha* and *Mor-Rioghan*. This is borne out by the fact that a banshee comes as one of the three: a young beautiful woman, a stately matron and a crone. Banshees are usually described as being dressed in white, such as a "winding sheet" or grey such as a hooded cloak, with long, fair hair. That long, fair hair is supposedly brushed with a silver comb, but Patricia Lysaght (Associate Professor of the Irish studies program at University College in Dublin who wrote the book: *The Banshee: The Irish Death Messenger*) pointed out that this is possibly confused with the local mermaid myths. In Scotland, the *bean nighe* or "washer-woman" usually shows up washing the blood stained clothes of those about to die. A banshee can also appear as an animal form such as a crow, hare or other animals associated with witchcraft. Some traditions indicate that a banshee could be the ghost of a woman who was either murdered or died in childbirth.

The other unique aspect about the banshee is its wailing cry which heralds the death of someone. The description of the wail varies in that according to tradition, if a banshee loves those she calls, it will be a soft, tender, soothing chant and if she hates, it would be a fiendish sound. Other descriptions include a piercing wail that can shatter glass or a thin, screeching sound. Sometimes only one person would hear it and other times, everyone, including neighbors, may hear the wail. Although there is belief that the banshee is foretelling the inevitable and paying her respects, her appearance is met with dread. A note of interest is that traditionally when an Irish village citizen died, a woman would sing a lament at their funeral and these woman singers are sometimes referred to as "keeners" or *caoineadh* and were in much demand.

To this day, banshees have an equal footing with the fairies and the leprechauns in Irish folklore and even are used in modern literature, most notably the Harry Potter series by J.K. Rowling. Should you be of Irish or Scottish descent, it seems to be an inevitable conclusion that you will hear a banshee wail warning you of a death in the family and an experience you will never forget as many Celtic folk have testified since the 8th century.

Beast of Bray Road

A lonely patch of road near Delavan and Elkhorn in Wisconsin is said to be the home of a strange wolf-like beast. There have been tales throughout the world of werewolves, but the Beast of Bray Road has been seen right up to the current day. Encounters with werewolves were not uncommon in Wisconsin and began to occur in 1936. But it is recent sightings of the beast that has the locals living in fear.

The beast is a hairy humanoid with prominent canine features. The beast is often seen lingering near Bray Road in Southeastern Wisconsin. It will sometimes be seen walking upright on two legs (bipedal), but it has also been seen running on all fours. It has the face of a wolf but the body of a muscular and hairy man. Eyewitness reports of the beast place it at about 6 feet in height.

The beast has pointed ears and three long claws on each hand/paw. The one feature that sets it aside from other unidentified creatures is the long dog-like muzzle of the beast. It has been reported by witnesses to be comparable to that of a German Shepard or a wolf.

While the eyewitness accounts of the beast seem to be on the increase, there is one thing that seems to stand out in them all which is the cold and calculating stare of the beast. When a vehicle travels down the road, witnesses often note that the beast's eyes seem to glow with an eerie yellow luminescent light when struck by the shine from headlights.

With eyewitness accounts of bipedal hairy apes abounding in North America, the Beast of Bray Road is considered by some to be a Bigfoot and not a werewolf at all, but this view stands in contrast with each of the countless eyewitness reports of the beast. Out of all werewolf legends worldwide, the Beast of Bray Road is the best documented account of what may be an actual werewolf type of creature. There have been numerous media reports on the beast and even a low budget movie based on it.

Just as there are many sightings of the beast, there are equally as many proposed explanations for what it is. Some are as simple as a case of misidentification of actual wolves or large dogs. While others link it to a series of pranks and hoaxes, the only problem with the hoax explanation is that the pranksters would have to have been alive and perpetrating such a prank since the mid-1930's.

The first of the most recent wave of sighting of the beast occurred on October 31, 1999. While driving down Bray Road near Delavan, Doristine Gipson hit something with her car. Worried, she stopped her car and got out to investigate. When she got out of the car, she did not find anything lying in the road behind her car, so she started to look around to see if she had hit an animal that tried to crawl off the road. As she turned to look off the road she was shocked to find a pair of yellow eyes peering back at her. At that instant, the form began to move toward her from about 50 feet away. Gipson was not able to make out clear details in the darkness, but she was able to notice the outlined form of something large and hairy.

Afraid of the oncoming creature, Gipson turned and quickly retreated to the safety of her car. Once inside she began to leave the area, but as she did, the beast jumped onto the trunk of her car. She accelerated and the beast was unable to hold on and fell to the road. Shaken but still curious, she returned to the scene later that night. When she arrived back at the scene, she had a child with her in the car. As she stopped the car and peered out the window she once again noticed the large dark form on the side of the road. As the figure started to move in her direction, she told the child that was with her to lock her car door just prior to putting the car in gear and speeding away once again.

The following day she told a neighbor about the incident and showed her neighbor the scratches on her car. Gipson was not sure what she had struck, but suspected that she may have hit a bear. The events of Gibson's encounter began to quickly spread and soon more and more people began to come forward with their stories involving an encounter with the Beast of Bray Road, some dating back as long as 1989.

With speculation and sarcasm running wild among researchers and the general public the question will remain unanswered until someone is able to get some valid evidence of the creature. To date, hard evidence is lacking, but the local tales seem to be growing in number. It is very possible that the entire story could be just a story intended to increase tourist traffic in the area to bolster a town's economy or it could be an elaborate hoax by some locals looking for a good laugh. With no hard evidence, such as foot castings, hair samples, photos or video it is likely that this elusive beast may remain a part of local lore and legend until it is captured on film. One thing is certain, and that is that sightings of the Beast of Bray Road have subsided and the trail grown cold for the time being.

Bermuda Triangle

For some, the name Bermuda Triangle can be confusing because it is sometimes referred to as the Devil's Triangle. It is a patch of Earth that sits on one of the deepest and sporadic pieces of the Atlantic Ocean known as the Puerto Rican Trench. The chronicles of its dark waters date back to the time of Christopher Columbus, but it was not until the strange disappearance of the U.S. Navy's flight 19 that it earned it place in the world of unexplained phenomena.

Disappearances of ships, boats and aircraft have all been reported in the area and have been attributed to everything from interdimensional portals, gas bubbles, water spouts and UFOs to the lost city of Atlantis. The boundaries of the triangle vary and are in fact more of a quasi-trapezoid based on the reported disappearances. The most familiar triangular boundary starts off the coast of Miami then points to San Juan, Puerto Rico then goes to the Islands that neighbor the Bahamas. The majority of the disappearances have occurred in the region of the triangle between the Bahamas and the Florida Straits. In spite of the mysterious, strange and unexplained disappearances in the Bermuda Triangle Lloyd's of London, the well known insurance company has determined the region is no more dangerous than any other part of the ocean and charges normal rates for boaters wishing to insure their vessels in the region.

However, there is one case that cost the United States a loss totaling several million dollars, which was the case of Flight 19, a training mission of five TBM Avenger bombers that took off from Ft. Lauderdale, Florida on December 5, 1945. The flight was headed by Lt. Charles C. Taylor, an experienced naval pilot. The skies were clear that day as the flight took off, but things soon started to go wrong as their compasses began to malfunction and the skies became stormy by the time the flight crew was able to make its final radio transmission before losing radio contact and disappearing into history forever. The official Navy report of the incident attributes the loss of Flight 19 to "causes or reasons unknown."

Bible Code

Discovered by an Israeli mathematician named Eliyahu Rips and his colleagues, Yoav Rosenberg and Doron Witztum, the trio declared that the Hebrew Bible contains secret encrypted messages that give clues and warnings as to the future of mankind. The code had been known to a few rabbis over the past few centuries, but it was not until the trio decided to use modern computer technology to unlock its secrets that the full scope of the code would be revealed. The sum of their research was brought to public attention on 1997 by Michael Drosnin whose book, *The Bible Code*, made the bestseller lists.

They ran test after test to determine if their results were consistent and in each case, they achieved the same results. They found people, places and inventions that did not exist at the time the Bible was first written which did not exist for centuries to come. They started their search by arranging all of the 304,805 letters in the Hebrew Bible and the Torah into a select pattern. They removed all the spaces between words and the punctuation. Once they had managed to put the two texts into one continuous string they entered the string into the computer and told it to look in every direction for matches for names, words, and phrases. What appeared in every direction were words and phrases.

To further test their theory, they told the computer to pick out the name of some of the more important rabbis that had been mentioned prominently in the Hebrew texts. Again, the computer performed perfectly and the computer not only located the names of the rabbis, but it also found the dates of their births and deaths within the same few pages of the text.

But names and dates of biblical figures were not the only things that they found in the code. Just prior to the onset of the first Gulf War, the group found a message hidden in biblical text that warned of the start of the Gulf War. The message read "fire on 3rd Shevat," the exact day that Saddam Hussein launched his scud missiles at Israel (January 18th). Close by that message they also found the words Hussein and scuds all within close by pages of the book of Genesis.

Michael Drosnin is the only researcher of the Bible code that is an agnostic and a journalist. While researching the Bible code, he remained impartial until the Prime Minister of Israel, Yitzhak Rabin, was shot and killed by an assassin's bullet in 1995, which was something that Drosnin had read in the Bible code he was researching a year earlier. But, with the many cases that support the validity of the Bible code, there are still those that attempt to play it down and discredit it.

To help establish the validity of their claims, the

group of researchers used a Hebrew copy of *War and Peace* as a control. When they performed the same scans on *War and Peace*, they only found random words which lent credit to the potential that there was a hidden code in the Bible and Torah. However, subsequent test of a similar nature have been performed on Moby Dick and, as with the Bible, it too produced prophetic results. With more testing needed and time being the ultimate proof, it is likely that only those who place their belief in the Bible Code will benefit from what it has to offer.

Black Helicopters

Since the 1980's there have been hundreds of reports from all over the country involving strange black helicopters that seem to appear at locations that involve UFO activity. They show up as black unmarked helicopters that harass UFO witnesses. They also have been seen at the scene of cattle mutilations throughout the country. The pilots are usually dressed in all black with no visible insignia on their uniforms.

The exact reason for their appearance is never made clear, but they are suspected as being a part of the infamous Men In Black that often show up to harass and quiet UFO witnesses. According to some investigators, the mission of these dark helicopter crews is to use any means necessary to hide the activities of UFOs on Earth.

It has been suggested by some investigators that they are a part of a secret government that operates outside of the norm. It has been suggested that their goal is to abduct civilians and subject them to mind control experiments like those carried out in the 1950 and 1960 under the project name MK-ULTRA. Once they have achieved their goals, they return the unsuspecting victim with a memory of an alien abduction scenario to discredit the victims' story.

The strange and unmarked aircraft are often seen in locations suspected of hiding secret underground installations and underground bases. Whether or not the strange helicopters are a part of some secret government project or are actively involved in the cover up of UFO activity, their presence is a very real one that has been noted by hundreds of men and women each year. When the Federal Aviation Administration was asked to investigate the black aircraft, it said that it was not conducting an investigation of the black unmarked helicopters. But, witnesses to the strange craft reported being questioned later by the same FAA panel who claimed not to be conducting investigations. Regardless of their true purpose, any organization or government that has to operate in secret when dealing with its own people is usually not up to any good. The truth behind these helicopters will not be known until one goes down in public or is seen by a large population all at once.

Blood Countess

Of all of the terrifying characters in history, there is one that stands out in a category all her own which is that of a real life "vampire" female with a lust for blood that makes Vlad Dracul Tepes, the original Dracula, pale in comparison. Countess Elizabeth Balthory (1560-1614) was a Transylvanian noblewoman that became known as the "Blood Countess" as a result of her seemingly endless taste for human blood. She not only drank the blood of her innocent young maids, but also bathed in their blood as well.

She was born to powerful nobles and was an arrogant and temperamental child that became a ruthless adult. She gave birth to her first child at the tender age of 14. She was married a year later at the age of 15 to a count by the name of Ferencz Nadasdy who was very wealthy and several years older than she was. While her life seemed normal at first, it would soon change forever.

After being married to the count, she went to live at the family estate located at the Castle Savar. She tended to her duties, hosting parties and receptions for her fellow nobles as expected, smiling and putting on a happy face in front of them, but secretly degrading and terrorizing her servants in private. Her sadistic behavior toward her young servants would continue to become worse as time passed. It was not uncommon for the nobles at that time in the region to be treated as virtual kings and queens to be granted anything that they desired without question.

From the very start, Countess Balthory seemed to take special pleasure in tormenting the young servant girls who attended her. One of her favorite punishments for the servant girls, who did wrong, was to place oiled paper between their toes and set it on fire. This tortuous technique of discipline was taught to Balthory by her husband and was known as "star-kicking," so named after the wild jerking and jumping movements that the girls made as the fire scorched their feet.

Aside from her sadistic behavior towards her servants, Balthory began to grow concerned about growing old and losing her beauty. By the age of 25, she had lost her husband to death and feared that the same would happen to her if she did not take action to prevent it. Already partaking of the dark arts of sorcery she had participated in secret sacrifices of animals, it was just a matter of time before Balthory took the next step into darkness by sacrificing a living, breathing human being.

Her opportunity for such sacrifice came sooner rather than later. One evening while being attended by one of her servants, the maid became clumsy and to punish her, Balthory picked up a pair of scissors and struck the young attendant across the face. When the blade struck the woman, she began to bleed with some of the blood splashing onto Balthory's hand. Seeing the blood on her hand Balthory began to suspect that it somehow made her skin appear younger. From that day forward she began to bathe in blood of young maidens from the nearby village by taking them into her home as servants, never to be heard from again.

Once in her charge, the girls would be tortured, bled and eventually killed. She would have the young girls tied up tightly so she could enjoy watching the blood as it spurted from their veins before bathing in their blood and drinking it. On some occasions Balthory would even go so far as to force some of the girls to eat the flesh of those who she had already killed.

This real life blood-drinking sadistic monster would eventually be caught when she ran out of peasant girls to use for her nightmarish beauty treatments. Left with nowhere else to turn, she began to take the daughters of the other nobles as her victims. It was at that point that the Lady Balthory was caught and eventually imprisoned for her horrors by being walled up in her own bedroom at the castle Csejthe. She had ventilation and was permitted to live out her days in the seclusion where nobody would ever cast eyes on the beauty she so desired to maintain. The life of the would-be queen of the damned came in 1614 when she died suddenly and alone in her one-room prison.

C

Castle Poenari

A castle in the foothills of the Carpathian Mountains currently in ruins, that has earned a place in history, mystery, haunting and legend, it stands on the isolated spot where it was built just 20 miles from the former capital of Wallachia. The castle stands overlooking the Arges River near Poenari, Romania, like a vulture standing watch over its dying prey. A fitting and desolate reminder of the atrocities that once took place there, built in its final form on the backs of peasants, the castle holds testimony to the terrors of one of history's greatest antiheros.

The castle itself dates to the 14th century but debate rages on as to whether or not it was actually built in the 12th century. The castle itself is best known as "Dracula's Castle." When work was to be done on the castle, Prince Vlad Tepes, also known also as Vlad Dracul, invited his political enemies, the Boyars, to the castle for a lavish Easter feast. He instructed his guests to bring their families with them. When they arrived at the castle the feast began. There was music and merriment and when his guests had had their fill, he ordered his guards to take his guests prisoner. He had the Boyars and their wives taken out and impaled on stakes, hence his nickname "Vlad the Impaler." He then turned his anger and hatred for them towards their children. Anyone in good health was put to work rebuilding the aging castle. His prisoners worked on the castle in the same clothes that they had come to feast in. So vast in numbers were his victims that they formed a human chain from the town of Poenari all the way to the remote castle.

The members of the Turkish army were also impaled on the stakes at the castle and were so numerous onlookers referred to the scene as a forest of human bodies.

Vlad Tepes and his castle were also the inspiration for Bram Stoker's infamous and brooding novel "Dracula."

The castle fell into ruins over the centuries, but in the 1970's efforts were made to bolster the failing communist economy through tourism. The castle was once again opened up to visitors, but even to this day it receives few due to its remote location. Descendents of some of Vlad's enemies have attempted to visit the castle and were met with injury and eventual death. One of the best known researchers of Vlad Dracul is Radu Florescu, who is one of the descendents of Vlad's fiercest enemies. Florescu had researched the history and life of Dracula since the 1960's and it was his father that met with harm while attempting to climb to the castle in the 1960's. Florescu is so troubled by the events of his family history and that of Dracula that even to this day he will not spend time in the castle. Other investigators have reported strange lights and sounds while staying in the castle at night, but given all of the horrors that transpired on that lonely piece of Earth it would not be surprising if there were more to the legend of Dracula's Castle than just rocks.

Cattle Mutilations

Often thought by veterinarians and officials to be nothing more than the work of predators, the strange phenomena of cattle mutilations continues to plague ranchers throughout the United States. The phenomena have come to be known as bovine excision and involve the mutilation of cattle and other livestock under unusual circumstances. Reports of the strange mutilations began to surface in the early 1960's and have taken a steady incline over the following years. By the mid 1970's there were report of cattle mutilations in over 15 states.

So prevalent were the mutilations by 1975 that Senator Floyd Haskell contacted the FBI and asked for an investigation. By that time 130 mutilations had been reported in the state of Colorado alone. To date, there has been more than a million dollars in lost livestock to the strange and still unexplained phenomena.

The mutilations themselves often involve some of the same characteristics regardless of their geographic location. Mutilated animals are often found with their eyes, udders and sexual organs removed. In most cases, other soft tissue is found missing as well, like the anus, along with 12 inches of intestines. Tongue, lips, ears and the soft tissue of the lower body are also missing when the animals are discovered.

When found, the animals are often discovered to be missing parts of the jaw and contain surgical incisions. What makes the event so strange is that there is never a clear cause of death and none of the remaining organs of the body are abnormal in any way. With most debunkers claiming predation, it is odd that the animals have no physical signs of predation. In fact, most predators have been observed avoiding the areas where the mutilations occur.

While some cases seem to be nothing more than natural causes, others are so profound that they cannot be explained by natural means. In at least one instance the mutilated body of a cow was found 50 feet up in a tree with all of the classic signs of bovine excision. While the public is told that the cattle have died of natural causes and that their mutilations are the sole result of predators, the dark truth may be found in the fact that all of the mutilated animals are from a specific age rage between 4 and 5 years old.

According to pathologists who have examined the mutilated carcasses, the incisions left on the animals appears to have been made with some type of advanced laser technology. Veterinarians that stand in support of an alternative explanation have noted that the majority of the animals have been fully drained of their blood prior to death. They have also noted complete vascular collapse in most of the specimens, something that is not possible by known technology.

Champ

A North American cousin to the famous Loch Ness Monster, the first reported sighting of the creature is uncertain, but legend has it that the first European account was made by a French explorer in 1609 by the name of Samuel de Champlain, for whom the lake is named after. According to accounts, he saw the creature while fighting the Iroquois along the bank of the lake. Unfortunately, Champlain's account was never documented and still remains unconfirmed.

With Champlain's account left up to rumor and legend, there are older accounts of the creature's existence that come from the Native American Iroquois and Abenaki tribes. In the late 19th century, P.T. Barnum offered a $50,000 reward to anyone that could produce the body of Champ. Since then, both Vermont and New York have enacted laws placing the cryptid on their endangered species list, but the lake also borders Ontario, Canada which does not recognize the animal's existence.

One of the most famous sightings of the creature occurred in 1883. A local Sheriff, Nathan Mooney, was standing on the shore when he spotted the creature about 50 yards offshore. He noticed that it had what he described as, "round white spots inside its mouth" and that "the creature appeared to be about 25 to 30 feet in length." Following his sighting, there were many other witnesses that began to come forward with their reports. What makes Sheriff Mooney's sighting so important is that it actually predates public awareness of the Loch Ness Monster by 50 years.

While there are a number of photos of ripples and wakes in the water of the lake, there is one photo that still stands out as one of the most credible photos of the creature ever taken. It was taken in 1977 by local resident Sandra Mansi who was standing on the edge of the lake with her family when she suddenly noticed the creature emerge from the water just offshore. The picture is so clear that it shows what some claim is a plesiosaur, a prehistoric aquatic reptile, not a dinosaur. Experts that have examined the Mansi photo have concluded that it has not been tampered with in any way and that it shows an actual object of some kind.

Chupacabra

Known as the "Goat Sucker" in its native Puerto Rico, the creature is small but vicious. This cryptid animal, unknown to modern science, originated on the small island and became a part of the unexplained world in 1975 when stories about a series of farm animals being killed on the island began to surface in the small town of Moca where it was first called El Vampiro de Moca (The Vampire of Moco). The name Chupacabra is credited to Puerto Rican comedian Silverio Perez who first coined the term.

Eyewitnesses began to describe this strange creature as about three to four feet tall and gray in color. Often times, resembling eyewitness descriptions of small gray aliens, they are reported to have large and disproportionate heads with large oval shaped eyes, a mouth full of sharp teeth, and a row of spikes on its back. Eyewitnesses will sometimes report a foul sulfuric odor associated with the creature.

The first reports of the creature began to surface around the mountainous interior of Puerto Rico, where villagers began to find the carcasses of goats, sheep, cows, chickens and other farm animals completely drained of their blood. Local authorities maintain that the deaths are the result of attacks by stray dogs and other animals that have been illegally introduced to the island. The director of Puerto Rico's Department of Agriculture Veterinary Services Division claims that the killings might be the result of a fanatical religious sect that has been using the animals for religious sacrifices.

Since initial reports from Puerto Rico the creature has been reported in Mexico, Chile, Colombia, Honduras, El Salvador, Nicaragua, Panama, Peru, Brazil, the Dominican Republic, Bolivia, Argentina, and parts of the United States to include New Mexico, Texas, Southern California and Miami. The creature's presence seems to focus on Latin American communities. Some members of those communities liken the creature to stories of the boogie man, while others swear that the creature is very real and very dangerous.

Several accounts of the creatures being killed have been recorded. In most instances they turn out to be nothing more than coyotes or dogs with mange. A classic case occurred in 2004 when a San Antonio rancher killed a hairless dog-like animal that had attacked his livestock. The animal's body was subjected to DNA testing at UC Davis, which determined the animal to be nothing more than a coyote with sarcoptic mange.

The theory that the mysterious creature is most likely a dog with mange seems to be supported by most of the eyewitness descriptions which describe the animal as having a reptile like appearance. Its skin is described as leathery, scaly, greenish or gray. Most canines with mange do have a "scaly" or leathery like skin, but other canine medical conditions, like severe flea bite dermatitis can cause the same type of appearance.

One explanation for what the Chupacabra may be has been presented by the people of Puerto Rico. There is a large U.S. Military presence on the island and it has long been rumored that the creature may actually be an escaped or failed genetic test by the government, a genetic mutant if you will. Advocates of this concept call the creature an Anomalous Biological Entity (ABE). The problem with this concept is that it does not account for the creature's presence in other parts of the world.

Coral Castle

Located just north of Homestead, Florida, this oddity stands as a testament to one man's undying love and to the mysterious powers of the universe itself. A small man in stature, Ed Leedskalnin, stood only five feet tall and weighed less than one hundred pounds. What makes Leedskalnin's story and work so remarkable is that he managed to build a literal castle out of natural coral without the use of mechanical equipment or assistance from any other living human being.

Born in 1887, his story began in his homeland of Riga, Latvia. It was on the day before he was to be wed to his fiancée that Ed would be left with a heartbreak that he would take to his grave. On that day his would-be fiancée, the young sixteen-year old Agnes Scuffs, would have a change of heart. Torn by heartbreak, Ed left his home country and eventually ended up in South Florida in 1918.

Once he arrived in Florida City, he purchased a piece of land and set out to build himself a home that was to be designated a monument to his lost love Agnes. He began to cut out large pieces of coral stone using nothing more than wedges, saws, block and tackle, rope and a wagon that he had pieced together from parts he gathered from a local junk yard. He set out building his monument under the cover of darkness in total secrecy. Working alone, he was mysteriously able to move coral stones that weighed an average of 9 tons without the aid of mechanical tools, cranes or electricity. When his castle was completed, Ed had managed to move a total of 1,100 tons of coral rock on his own, the heaviest of which weighed 35 tons.

After he completed his monument to Agnes, he began to grow displeased with Florida City and decided to move the entire structure by himself to its current location just outside of Homestead, Florida. Ed took the castle apart in secret and transported it piece by piece on a borrowed tractor to its new location.

The big mystery is just how this small man was able to accomplish such a feat by himself. Ed never left any records as to how he managed to quarry and move the massive stones. What is known about Ed is that he spent many hours during the day resting and reading about cosmic energy, science, astronomy and the Egyptian pyramids. Ed was a firm believer in the fact that our modern concept of magnetism was wrong. He believed that all matter consists of individual magnets and that it is the movement of those magnets within matter that produces magnetism and electricity.

Many people have tried to uncover the secret to Ed's methods, but nobody has succeeded to date. What is clear in his methods is that a simple block and tack would not support the weight of the immense stones without some other means of manipulation. Not just moving enormous coral stones, Ed's castle features an outdoor oven that does not use electricity, a 9 ton gate that can be opened with a single finger, a telescope that points directly at the North Star, a sun dial, perfectly balanced rocking chairs, and coral beds with pillows that are as comfortable as any modern bed available. Even with all of our modern technology, we are still unable to explain his methods. In 1986 the nine-ton stone gate had to be repaired and it required several weeks and a fifty-ton crane to do what Ed Leedskalnin did by himself.

Never giving up hope that his long lost love Agnes would come to see her tribute, Ed eventually passed away in 1951, taking with him his secrets. Since his death the current owners of the castle were eventually able to locate Agnes and invite her to see the monument that Ed built for her. She declined, saying that she was aware of it, but had no interest in it. But despite her lack of interest in it, the mystery of the Coral Castle continues and its ability to withstand hurricanes and time have proven it to be a true wonder inspired by lost love.

Crop Circles

In the late 1970's strange circles began to appear in crop fields in England and quickly became a worldwide phenomena, but the appearance of such strange geometric shapes in fields across the world has been going on since as early as 1678. At the time they were identified with "corn fairies" and appeared in wheat fields in Scotland. Since the modern era of the Crop Circle, as they have become known, the phenomena has actually been traced back as early as medieval times throughout Europe and Scandinavia.

In 1991, two retired artists from England came forward and claimed that they were responsible for creating the mysterious crop circles using nothing more than a board and a rope. While their confession seemed to explain some of the simpler crop circles that had appeared during that time frame, they did not explain all of the circles that had been made throughout history. Since that time, there have been others who have created the circles, but there are still a number of crop circles that cannot be accounted for, such as those that appear in deserts, icy regions and other remote locations.

The phenomenon has become so prevalent that an entire group of researchers known as cerealogists has sprouted up to study it. They have determined that since 1989 there have been over two hundred formations a year in the United Kingdom alone. They have also been able to determine that those circles without an explanation have also been altered inexplicably, either biochemically or biophysically.

The strange formations have been attributed to everything from ball lighting to UFOs. Strange lights have often been observed at the sight of crop circles, but no definite proof exists as to their cause. One of the more prominent theories as to what causes the circles has to do with a strange natural phenomena known as a plasma vortex. Some researchers have even attributed the increasing complexity of the designs to a form of sacred geometry that is being used by some higher intelligence to communicate with us through a form of harmonic resonance. Dr. Simeon Hein, a crop circle researcher, is an advocate of this theory and claims that the circles are "tuned in" to a specific harmonic that gives them unusual properties to affect humans, from healing to increased libido.

With some of the circles made by known pranksters and artists, others are not so easy to explain away. Their unusual properties and strange effects do seem to have an impact on human beings, whether it is real or psychological will most likely remain a subject of debate as the circles continue to make their mark on this planet.

D

Dead Sea Scrolls

Discovered in a cave near Qumran, Israel in 1945, the scrolls may hold the secret untold truth to both the Jewish and Christian religions. Believed to have been written by the Jewish sect known as the Essenes, the scrolls have been directly linked to both major religions. Some scholars contend that the concepts taught by Jesus are not exclusive to the Christian faith, but actual fundamental doctrines of some sects of Jews during the time of Jesus. They offer the Dead Sea Scrolls as evidence of the link between the changing tides of Judaism in parallel to the formation of Christianity.

Author Herschel Shanks claims that the scrolls bring into question, "the naïve notion that Jesus' Jewishness was accidental or incidental and the belief that his message was wholly new, unique and unrelated to anything that had gone before, astonishing everyone who heard it."

It was not until after the Roman destruction of Jerusalem in 70 C.E. that the all of the various Jewish sects began to disappear and take on their modern Jewish doctrine. Basically, the Dead Sea Scrolls offer us a view of history that offers us a more realist version of two major religions. Rather than being very different, the scrolls tell us that both Judaism and Christianity were at one time primarily one in the same until the Romans altered both religions forever.

One of the most mysterious of all the scrolls that falls under the general label of the "Dead Sea Scrolls" is a scroll found in 1952, seven years after the first scrolls were found, by a team of Jordanian and French archaeologists. The scroll was engraved on copper and was very badly damaged. In order to try to translate the scroll it had to be cut into twenty-three pieces because it was too fragile to unroll. Translation has been a slow process and over 50 years later the total contents have yet to be revealed, but what has been translated has managed to present more questions than answers.

The copper scroll seems to indicate hints as to the location of biblical treasures. The scroll list sixty-four tons of silver and twenty-five tons of gold, but that is more silver and gold than would have been able to be mined for the entire world at the time. This fact alone has left scholars puzzled as to how it is that the scroll lists more silver than could be mined for the entire planet at the time. Could this piece of the Dead Sea Scroll be the treasure map that points to King Solomon's Mine?

Devil's School

Designed by Rutledge Holmes and built in 1917, the school was named the Riverside Park School and was the first public elementary school built in the city of Jacksonville, Florida. Today it stands as a crumbling and condemned old building that is off limits to the public. But this seemingly ordinary pile of brick and rubble holds more than its fair share of mystery. It has become known to the locals as the "Devil's School" and it is said that it is one of the most haunted places in the area.

The tales of hauntings at the school began in the 1960's when a furnace exploded killing a janitor, several teachers and half of the students. After the school was repaired and reopened, strange events started to occur. They became so prevalent that the teachers began refusing to work at the school.

But the strange events that started to occur at the

school after the furnace explosion were only a small part of what earned this place its name.

The principal of the school was its most notorious character and the reason that it earned its place in infamy within the town. According to accounts from the time when the school was active, students who would be sent to the principal's office would never be heard from again. The disappearances were eventually attributed to the school's principal, who was discovered to be a cannibal. Apparently he had turned a closet in his office into a meat locker where he would store the bodies of his student victims until he feasted on their flesh.

Eventually the school was closed and fell into ruin when it began to be used by a group of local devil worshipers whose ritualistic graffiti could still be seen as late as 2000. The building was officially condemned in the 1970's and a fire broke out in it in 1995. The windows were boarded up and a chain link fence was put up to keep out trespassers. Plans are currently on the drawing board to convert the building into condominiums as part of an urban renewal project. The project is not being rushed and is currently still pending. Perhaps the dead are not ready to part with their home.

Dragon's Triangle

Like its twin in the Atlantic Ocean, this mysterious area of the Pacific Ocean is known for the countless number of strange and unexplained disappearances that occur there each year. If one were to take a giant pencil and run it through the Earth starting at the Bermuda Triangle, it would come out on the other side of the planet in the Dragon's Triangle.

The Dragon's Triangle follows the basic outline

from just North of Tokyo to about 145 degrees east latitude. It then heads west southwest past the Bonin Islands and down to Guam and Yap. It continues on west toward Taiwan and eventually heads back to Japan.

While the west was well aware of the mysterious disappearances of the Bermuda Triangle throughout the 20th century, it was not until the late 1960's that the west became aware of the similarities between it and the Dragon's Triangle. One of the major reasons for the delay in comparison was WWII, language problems and postwar racist attitudes in the west. It is interesting that prior to the 1960's, there were some of the highest number of disappearances that occurred in the region.

During 1952-54 the nation of Japan lost a total of five military vessels and their crews without explanation. The number of people lost on those five vessels totaled over 700. The Japanese government was so concerned by the losses that it actually funded a study to investigate the region and sent a ship into the area with over 100 scientists on board. Their results were inconclusive and they were unable to locate a specific cause for the disappearances.

Dybbuk

While most traditions have tales of vampires, demons and ghosts, there is one tradition that blurs the lines between the three. In the Hebrew tradition, there is an ambivalent creature that seems to draw of the characteristics of all three entities, known as a Dybbuk. Though not well-known, there existed an early belief among the early Hebrews that some people could magically draw strength from others threw being near or touching them. Often time the old or frail would be laid beside the young to draw vitality from them.

The belief was so strong that there actually exists a biblical account of such a vampire-like extraction of energy in the book of Kings 1-4. (Albeit watered down in the King James Version):

"Now King David was old and stricken in years and they covered him with clothes but he got no heat. Wherefore his servants said unto him, "Let there be sought for my lord the king, a young virgin and let her stand before the king and her cherish him and let her lie in they bosom, that my lord the king may get heat."

So they sought for a fair damsel throughout all the coast of Israel and found Abishag a Shummanite and brought her to the king. And the damsel was very fair and cherished the king and ministered to him but the king knew her not."

In the biblical version the frail and aging king is offered a young virgin to lie with, but not know carnally, to regain his energy and strength, something that would allow him to deal with the threats from his enemies. The specific traits of the Dybbuk are not very clear and can often become confused with those of demons or ghosts. What is clear is that just like demons in the Christian religion, the Dybbuk has the ability to possess living human beings and the Rabbis were once very concerned with protecting the innocent from being consumed by them.

When a person became possessed by a Dybbuk, they would go into a type of seizure and start to act out of character. One such tale of a Dybbuk from the Christian Bible is that of Jesus casting the demons into the swine.

While a Dybbuk could drain the living of strength and even possess them, it was how one became a Dybbuk in the first place that was the strangest of all, as it was this aspect of the Dybbuk that tied the belief in vampires, demons and ghosts all together. To become a clinging soul known as a Dybbuk, one had to die either without having atoned for one's sins, not been buried in accordance with Jewish ritual, cursed by a rabbi or someone who had committed suicide. Clearly the earliest foundations for what has become commonly known as the belief in vampires, demons and ghosts.

E

Easter Island

Located in the south eastern Pacific Ocean in the Polynesian island chain is a simple and quiet little island that is host to an army of strange and enigmatic stone warriors that seem to guard the island with their ever-watchful eyes. The island itself is actually an overseas territory of the nation of Chile.

The isolated little island sits on three extinct volcanoes and was first discovered by European visitors on Easter Sunday in 1722, hence its famous name. But it is not its name that has made this little piece of rock in the Pacific Ocean so famous, but an enduring mystery that surrounds its monumental statues known as moai. The moai were built by the island's original inhabitants the Rapanui, but what makes them so mysterious is that nobody has been able to figure out how or why they were built. The original people of the island were known to be cannibalistic and at the time of that the moai were built there were very limited natural resources available on the island, making their existence even more mysterious.

The number of moai of Easter Island totals 887. What the public knows as the moai are simply heads, but the truth is that full torsos have been unearthed beneath the huge heads. There have even been partially completed and discarded moai found in a distant quarry at a site known as Rano Raraku, indicating that their construction ended as suddenly as it began. The actual period of their construction varies, but seems to date somewhere between 1000 to 1700 B.C.E.

Amazingly, the Rapanui that created these amazing works were able to carve them and transport them without the use of metal or machinery. The only tools available to them were stone and wood, but wood was not an unlimited resource on a tiny isolated island. Out of all the moai created, only about three-quarters were placed in their current locations and the remainder were left somewhere along the way. To date, there have been fifty of the statues that have been re-erected in modern times using modern equipment and it turned out to be a very costly, labor intensive and time consuming endeavor using metal and modern technology.

The majorities of the great moai are very similar and seem to have the same appearance, but there are some that vary greatly like the Tukuturi that sits in a kneeling position and feature beards which is very unusual and uncommon for isolated Polynesian islanders. What makes this particular type of moai even stranger is its similarity to Indian stone statues found near Lake Titicaca in South America.

The Rapanui intended that the moai remain standing long after they were gone. A testament to that fact is the detail that they put into the construction of the foundations for these massive statues. Some sit atop an Ahu (platform) that consists of several layers of construction. The first platform is a retaining wall with a platform behind it. There are cushions of soft natural materials on the platform and a sloping ramp is set leading up to the cushion from the back side of the platform that is made from rounded boulders. There is a gravel-like pavement in front of the ramp and the Ahu itself is filled with rubble and debris. This amazing feat of construction was all done with an ancient understanding of basic construction and engineering. It leaves one to question whether or not we have truly advanced our engineering knowledge or if we have lost it along the way and are simply playing "catch up."

Eisenhower Meets ET

With the modern UFO era having begun in the 1940's it is no surprise that one of the most controversial figures in the UFO mystery is the then top U.S. government official, President Dwight D. Eisenhower. The entire story evolved from a letter written by Gerald Light of Los Angeles that was sent to Meade Laney, the director of Borderline Sciences Research Associates. The letter was dated April 16, 1954 and tells of how Light claimed to have returned from Muroc Dry Lake at the Edwards Air Force Base in California. Light stated in his letter that he was accompanied to Muroc by Franklin Allen of the Hearst newspapers, Bishop McIntyre of Los Angeles, and Edwin Nourse of the Brookings Institution.

Light further claims that the trio was invited to enter a restricted area at Edwards AFB and was shocked to see what he described as "otherplane aeroforms." Light said that he witnessed four very distinct and different types of crafts. His visit to the base lasted two days and during that time he claims that the crafts were being studied and handled by Air Force Officials with the full permission of their other-worldly occupants. Light referred to the aliens as "Etherians." Light also claimed that aside from the Air Force Officials present that then-President Eisenhower was also in attendance and was seen talking with the Etherians, Light expected Eisenhower to go public with the news that we are not alone in the Universe, but was shocked when that declaration never came.

While Light's story reads more like a Hollywood science fiction movie, his statements were corroborated in 1990 when a member of Great Britain's House of Lords, the Earl of Clancarty, came forward to offer the testimony of British pilot. The pilot was on vacation in Palm Springs in February of 1954 when he was called on by military officials and asked to go to Edwards AFB right away. When the pilot arrived at the base, he claimed to have seen aliens coming out of their ship and walk over to President Eisenhower, his entourage of officials and scientists. Lord Clancarty told how the pilot, whom he highly respected, described the aliens that were present at Edwards AFB. The pilot told Lord Clancarty that the aliens were able to breathe oxygen and were very much like humans in their height and appearance, but their features were misshapen. According to the pilot's version of the events, the aliens spoke English and very easily communicated with those present, particularly with Eisenhower, whom they wanted to start a program to educate and prepare the public for their open presence on Earth. Unfortunately, Eisenhower allegedly did not agree, citing how he feared the people of the world were not ready to accept the realization the extraterrestrials were present on Earth and operating in secret. He was concerned that this realization would cause widespread panic.

Electronic Voice Phenomena

The phenomenon is the manifestation of voices or sounds on some form of electronic media that are of a paranormal origin. Commonly associated with the talking dead, the voices are often unclear and inaudible to the naked ear, but in some case the recordings are so clear that they may be heard without the aid of amplification.

Unfortunately for paranormal investigators, the recordings are very limited in their content and often only contain a single word or two. Interest in the phenomena began as early as the 1940's when the term was introduced by the publishing company Colin Smythe Ltd. But the concept that the voices stemmed from the dead trying to reach out to the living was first introduced by photographer Attila Von Szalay. Szalay first attempted to record Electronic Voice Phenomena using a 78 rpm vinyl record, but it was not until the late 1950's that he was able to actually record disembodied voices using a reel-to-reel tape recorder. Today, the group that is most commonly associated with research in the phenomena is the American Association of Electronic Voice Phenomena which was founded by Sara Estep in 1982.

In recent years, the phenomenon has become an integral part of ghost investigations, but the actual phenomenon still remains unexplained. It has been attributed to other factors other than ghosts such as echoes from the past and sound waves that have traveled out into the upper atmosphere and bounced around for years, like a rerun of *I Love Lucy*. Other theories claim that the phenomena may be the result of subconscious psychokinesis on the part of paranormal investigators that are mentally geared for something to happen.

A Latvian psychologist by the name of Konstantin Raudive made over 100,000 recordings that he told listeners were from discarnate people. Some of the recordings were done in an RF-screened laboratory and contained identifiable words. To confirm his results, Raudive asks subjects to listen to and interpret the recordings for themselves. The results of his test showed that the subjects heard identical words on the recordings. As a result, Raudive concluded that the voices on the recordings could not be explained by normal means. He published the complete results of his work in his book, *Breakthrough – An Amazing Experiment in Electronic Communication with the Dead*'(1968, trans 1971).

The Department of Psychology at the University of Western Ontario conducted a series of EVP experiments in 1997. The project was headed by Imants Baruss. The experiments involved the methods used by Raudive in conjunction with those of Mark Macy. During over 81 sessions, a radio was tuned in to an empty frequency that created white noise. These sessions totaling 60 hours and 11 minutes were tape recorded while a participant sat in silence or asked a series of questions. The results of the experiment showed that the recordings were too few and too random to be deliberate contact.

Contrary to the results achieved by Baruss, the Society for Psychical Research, under the direction of Alexander MacRae, conducted their own experiment using a recording device of their own design in 2005. The device is very similar to what has become known as "the Box" and has been copyrighted under several names, but the creator of the device has long since disassociated himself from the device because he claimed it did not work as designed. Others have since latched on the device and still attempt to claim its validity, but without scientific validation. The device itself is actually based on old technology developed by Thomas Edison. To date, the best and most reliable means for experimenting with the phenomena is still the original method of using a standard recorder.

It was Thomas Edison that first attempted to create a device to call the dead and ended up creating the recorder. While we know what a recorder is, it is often overlooked that the reason we have these technologies is because a great thinker tried to experiment with Electronic Voice Phenomena before it existed as a widely accepted potential means of communication with the dead.

Elementals

Paranormal investigators mostly handle cases with ghosts or spirits of people (and animals) who have died and in rare situations, the so-called demonic or inhuman entities. However, there is another aspect of the paranormal world where you may come across the term an "elemental."

So what is an elemental? One interpretation of an elemental is "an ancient, either angry or malicious spirit" and this seems to be used by the standard ghost-hunter. Another interpretation used by occultists, neo-pagan or lightworkers define them as "nature spirits."

Paracelsus, a medical doctor who pioneered in use of chemicals and minerals in medicine, was one of the first to describe an elemental as a mythological being in his works on alchemy, but the belief of elementals itself may have started in a very early religion called animism. There are four types based on the elements of nature; earth, water, air and fire.

The traditional types are:

- Gnomes – earth elementals
- Undines – water elementals
- Sylphs – air elementals
- Salamanders – fire elementals

Gnomes usually live in the soil, under trees or rocks. They can help humans if they have been considerate of nature and treat it well. Gnomes can also help attract money and fulfill our material needs. When they take on form, it is usually short and stocky. Subgroups of gnomes include brownies, dryads, earth spirits, elves and satyrs.

Undines live in seas, fountains, waterfalls and lakes and are basically concerned with the movements of water and how they relate to human emotions. They are a beautiful and graceful, dressing themselves in shimmering and sea-colored garb. Undines can help us with our emotions, attract us to other people as well as developing our psychic abilities. Subgroups of undines include mermaids, oreads and naiads.

Sylphs are said to live on the tops of mountains and when taking on form, resemble cherubs or fairies with wings, although they are not considered to be real fairies. They are drawn to humans who use their minds, particularly in the creative arts, being the inspiration for human inventions and can help humans with our spiritual and mystical development.

Salamanders are considered the strongest elementals. Without them, fires cannot exist. They provide passion, motivation, will, courage and sexual prowess. They appear as sudden bursts of heat, but when taking on form, they primarily take on the form of a lizard.

In addition to these four standard types, there are also wood (fae), ether (human), metal (dwarf) and void (urisk). Elementals are present whenever practicing magick or are summoned otherwise. They are considered to be mischievous and like to play which may appear to us as threatening such as thunderstorms and raging seas, but the intent is for the definite purpose of being good for the planet as a whole.

According to Peter Aziz, a shaman, elementals can be invoked and encouraged to temporarily inhabit some object such as a mustika pearl or a bezoar stone, which can be obtained through websites dealing with such objects or even just being out in nature by meditating.

Basically, elementals are considered to be raw forces of nature that humans can ask for help, but not control and are another unique facet of the paranormal world to explore.

Extra Sensory Perception

Known as E.S.P., the phenomenon is the mental ability to acquire information independent of any known physical senses. This means that information obtained through Extra Sensory Perception is obtained through the use of the human mind alone. Its origins in public stem from a program that was a part of Duke University. Its results eventually became noticed by the United States government and were the original foundation for its top secret controlled remote viewing project during the cold war. The original tests in E.S.P. began as a result of the work of J.B. Rhine who wanted to attempt to determine the validity of mental abilities such as telepathy and sensing the thoughts of others.

The actual existence of the phenomenon still remains in question by mainstream science, but the very fact that the U.S. government helped fund the early work of Rhine indicates that its validity is something to be considered. Rhine's original work was carried out in the mainstream higher educational system at Duke University. It eventually separated itself from the university to become the Rhine Research Center, which is currently headed by Dr. Sally Rhine Feather, J.B. Rhine's daughter and one of his original test subjects.

During the 1930's Rhine and his wife Louisa attempted to develop physical research into the unexplained phenomenon of the mind. Often misunderstood as just the ability to read minds, Extra Sensory Perception actually encompasses a much larger group of individual mental abilities from clairvoyance and remote viewing to precognition, psychometry, clairvoyance, clairaudience, clairsentience, telepathy and even mediumship. J.B. Rhine's work in the field began by renaming the phenomenon "parapsychology" to avoid being confused with séances or false hauntings of the era. J.B. Rhine concentrated his efforts on actual laboratory studies while his wife Louisa devoted her research to collecting accounts from the field. The result of J.B. Rhine's work was the development of a test using a set of 5 cards with 25 cards to a pack. The cards were named after their designer and known as the Zener cards. Their design is very simple with a square, circle, 3 wavy lines, cross, and a star.

Zener cards are used in different ways test for different forms of ESP. For example, when testing for telepathy the "sender" looks at a series of cards and the "receiver" attempts to guess what symbol is on that card. When testing for clairvoyance the cards are hidden from everyone while the "receiver" attempts to guess what is on the cards without assistance from a "sender." In testing for precognition, the order of the cards is determined after the guesses are actually made. To ensure that the tests are random, the card were shuffled by hand and then by machine during the early days of testing, but today the entire process is done randomly by computer to ensure proper randomization.

An interesting study on Extra Sensory Perception was conducted to determine if hypnosis had an effect on an individual's ability to use E.S.P. Carl Sargent, a psychology major at the University of Cambridge, decided to investigate the reported link between the two. He recruited 40 students from the University to take part in his experiment. None of the 40 students that took part claimed to have any extra sensory ability or experience. Sargent then divided the group into a test group and a control group. The test group was hypnotized prior to being tested with a pack of Zener cards and the control group was not hypnotized prior to being tested with the Zener cards. The results were surprising and showed that subjects in the control group averaged about 5 out of 25 correct answers while the test group averaged much higher at 11.9 out of 25.

The only difference in the two groups was that the test group had been subjected to hypnosis and a higher relaxed state of consciousness prior to being tested with the cards. Results of ESP testing continue to vary, but there is significant evidence to show that those who believe in the phenomena do tend to score higher when tested, while those that do not believe in the phenomena tend to score at almost zero when tested. This indicates that a subject's mental state has a clear-cut effect on the outcome of their ability to affect extra sensory phenomena.

F

Face On Mars

In 1976, the Viking Orbiter made its way around the planet Mars sending back photographs to Earth of the planet's surface. Out of all the hundreds of photos that were sent back to NASA by the Mars orbiter, there is one series of photos that has set off a series of debates that continues to rage on to this day. The photos were taken of an area of Mars surface that is known as the Cydonia region and show what appears to be an artificial structure of a face on the otherwise barren surface of the red planet.

It is not the possible existence of such a structure that presents the biggest problem, but what such a structure would imply to humanity that has made it such a hot topic of debate for over 30 years now. A testament to the debate is Brian O'Leary who authored Mars 1999, has worked with Carl Sagan of Cornell University and was an Apollo astronaut, firmly believes that there is evidence of a civilization older than that of Earth's having once existed on Mars. His theories are supported by one of the best-known researchers on the subject, Richard C. Hoagland who has examined countless NASA photos and conducted numerous photo enhancements on those same photos.

Many of Hoagland's photo enhancements clearly show what appears to be a sphinx-like face on the surface of Mars near several pyramidal structures that are all located in the Cydonia region of the planet's surface. What makes the photos from the Cydonia region so strange is that they stand out in contrast to rest of the terrain of the entire surface. Lending support and credibility to Hoagland's work is the fact that he is a former consultant to NASA's Goddard Space Flight Center from 1975-1980.

When the original photos were released by NASA in 1976, there were a few frames that showed what looked like a face on the planet's surface, but were quickly accounted for as a trick of light by NASA officials. The entire subject might have been forgotten right there, but two of NASA's own engineers, Gregory Molenaar and Vincent DiPientro began to look at the pictures more closely. The entire controversy lays in whether or not the right side of the face is just a natural slope and the left side is just shadows cast by rock formations. Unfortunately, the bilateral symmetry of the formation is what causes most investigators to continue to pressure the space agency to investigate the region further.

Aside from the Sphinx-like face the other structures in the area also defy the terrain of the remaining surface of the planet. There are pyramids and what appear to be roadways with a city ruin in the area. Some have suggested that the objects are neither artificial or a trick of light, but the result of natural wind erosion on the planet's surface. In April of 1998, NASA received images of Mars from the Mars Global Surveyor of the Face that were much clearer than the original 1976 photos and showed nothing more than a pile of rocks and rubble, but did not take photos of the surrounding area and pyramids that were shown from the earlier photos. It has been suggested by proponents of the Face on Mars theory that the second attempt to photograph the face was deliberately set up to prove its non existence, very much like project blue book was set up to disprove the existence of UFO's.

What is intriguing is that NASA had an opportunity to settle the debate once and for all by having the Mars Lander land at Cydonia, but chose to avoid the location altogether, instead choosing a remote and isolated region of the Martian desert to make their first landing on the planet's surface.

Faerie Circles

A faerie or fairy circle is also known as fairy ring, elf circle or pixie ring and is very popular in folklore, particularly Scandinavian and Celtic folklore, as the place where fairies or elves could be found dancing or is an entry to the fairy or elf kingdom.

If a human steps into the ring, he or she runs the risk of either being carried off by or joining the fairies in their dancing which seems to occur for only a few minutes but lasts for seven years or more. The human could be rescued by someone who grab hold of his or her clothes. Another traditional way of avoiding being carried off by the faeries or elves is to run around the ring nine times.

Other traditions also refer to them as either the work of witches or devils, particularly in France and German

On the positive side, the Welsh believe that the faerie circles lead to fertility and fortune. If a house is built on one, the residents will prosper. If mountain sheep eat there, they would be more likely to flourish and be more bountiful than their counterparts on normal grass.

According to scientists, one theory is that faerie circles are caused by the spore of a fungus which can cause withering or color change in the grass. Another theory is that they could be created by a chain of mushrooms that are connected together.

One should note that those fungi can deplete the soil of nutrients, causing plant growing within the circle to become discolored. Other fungi produce hormone-like chemicals that affect plant growth, making them very luxuriant.

These theories could provide one of the reasons why cattle avoid them, not because they are inhabited by the faeries, according to legend!

There are apparently 40 to 60 mushroom species which grow in a circular pattern. Some mushrooms are actually edible, such as the Scotch bonnet. The largest mushroom circles are found in France and in southern England. The one in France is 800 meters in diameter and over 700 years old!

Fatima

Religious miracles have been a part of history since the beginning of time, but there is one such miracle that still haunts the hearts and minds of thousands of religious faithful. It occurred in the spring of 1917 and has come to be one of the greatest mysteries of faith to date. It was during that year that three young children in the mountain region of Portugal would claim to have seen a vision of the Virgin Mary for the first time, a vision that would be followed by six more.

Portugal was in the midst of fighting the "Great War" abroad and struggling with political turmoil at home. The government officials at the time were said to have been under the influence of Freemasonry and were allegedly not very sympathetic to religious beliefs of the region. In the small Catholic parish of Fatima, the children spent their time fulfilling their daily chores and delving into religious doctrine. It was no different for Lucia, Francisco and Jacinta, three ordinary children, who lived hard and difficult lives in a time of economic depression. Of the three children, it would be Lucia de Jesus that would take the legacy of Fatima to both the

Vatican and her grave.

When the trio first had their vision of the Virgin Mary, they were surprised, but being very loyal and devout believers, they attempted to tell their parents. What they quickly discovered was that the adults of their community were not so quick to believe the story of a few children.

The trio persisted and eventually the story began to spread and hundreds began to show up to see the vision of the Virgin Mary. As time passed and the story began to settle, the children went on their way and began their separate lives, but one chose to continue to pursue the messages that she received in 1917. Lucia decided to continue to follow her faith and joined the Roman Catholic sisterhood to become a nun.

She eventually ended up going to the Vatican where she shared the information that was given to her by the Virgin Mary with the Pope. What remains of the mystery is one final revelation that was supposed to have been revealed to the trio in 1917 and that final revelation is now since sealed in the vaults of the Vatican. With the passing of Lucia, the only way the world will know the truth is if the church verifies or denies it by opening up their secret files.

Fountain of Youth

One of the greatest mysteries of North America is Ponce de Leon's quest for the fountain of youth. Today, there is a location in St. Augustine, Florida that claims to be that fabled spring and charges admission for a paper cup and the privilege of a drink from the spring. There are actually several other springs that also claim to be the fountain of youth, two of which are actually Ponce de Leon springs in Florida, one in Volusia County and the other in Holmes County.

Interestingly, Ponce de Leon was only 39 years old when he began his search for the fountain of youth. While on a trip to Florida to search for gold, he had heard tales of the mysterious fountain prior to leaving Spain. Ponce de Leon's search for the fountain with the healing waters of life was not the only ones that indicate a long history of a strange fountain in the region with the miraculous powers to turn back the pages of time. The Indians that lived on the islands in the region usually referred to actual waters as a waterfall or river, but it was the Spanish that actually added the word spring to the story.

A Spanish historian by the name of Francisco Lopez de Gomara, wrote that Indians living on the island of Hispaniola had told him about a fountain with healing waters north of Cuba and Haiti. Unfortunately, there is no definitive proof that Ponce de Leon ever did find the Fountain of Youth, but there are some very strange and mysterious facts that do surround some of the springs in the area. The actual springs found in some parts of Florida are not only known to contain high levels of nutrients that help to maintain good health, but are also high in carbonates, boron, chromium, copper, gold, iodine manganese, fluoride, nickel, sea salt, sulfur, iron and magnesium. Florida is also home to the deepest spring in the world at a total depth of 200 feet, the Wakulla spring.

Aside from the natural properties of the springs found in Florida, there are census records of a St. Augustine family that all lived beyond 110 years of age. In fact one member of the family, Juan Gomez of Panther Key was around 120 years old at the time of his death and he did not die of natural causes, but was drowned. In 1996, the United States witnessed the passing of its oldest citizen, a Florida resident named Mary Thompson that died at the extended age of 120. So whether one believes that the fountain of youth exists or not, the fact remains that there is some substance to the exaggerated life-span of many residence of the region. So intriguing is the search for the fountain of youth that the well known magician, David Copperfield, has purchased an island in the Bahamas that he claims has a fountain that brings bugs back from the brink of death and makes dead flowers blossom. He is currently having the waters tested, but the island and the spring remain off-limits to the public.

G

Gandillon Werewolves

In 1598, there was a French family that came to be known as what may be the best known case for actual living werewolves. It involved a sister, brother, and two of the brother's children. It is alleged that they all roamed Jura ravaging the countryside and terrorizing its people. Pernette Gandillon was a simple poor girl who actually ran around on all fours, as if she was a wolf using her hands and arms as feet and legs. While it would seem to the modern observer that Pernette's condition was the result of a mental illness, it was not her habit of walking on all fours that caused the story to become one of the most documented in the annals of werewolves.

One day while having one of her "wolf" fits, Pernette ran across a brother and sister who were out playing and picking strawberries. Pernette suddenly attacked the girl and the girl's brother began to struggle with Pernette. The Brother tried to fight her off and eventually managed to fight her off with his knife. Pernette then turned her "werewolf's bloodlust" against the brother and managed to slash his neck with her uncut nails. Unfortunately, while the young boy was able to save his sister, he was not able to save himself from the fury of the lycan and the wound to his neck turned out to be fatal. When the girl returned home to tell what had happened, she identified Pernette as the beast who had committed the crime.

Villagers in the small town became enraged by the brutal death and formed a mob that tore Pernette to pieces in retaliation for the murder of the young boy. Shortly after Pernette was killed by the mob, her brother Pierre was accused of practicing witchcraft. The people of the village began to claim that he was kidnapping young children and take them to witches' Sabbat where he would transform himself into a wolf with long gray hair. Oddly, Pierre did not deny the charges, but proudly acknowledged that they were true and that while having transformed into the wolf he stated that he actually fed on animals and humans alike with great joy and pleasure.

Pierre's son Georges and his daughter Antoinette also confessed to similar behavior and crimes, but both Pierre and George had numerous scars on their faces and arms from dog bites and scratches that they had allegedly gotten while having take on a wolf's form. Eventually the remaining three Gandillons were tried and hanged and their bodies burned to put an end to curse of the Gandillon Werewolves once and for all. Following the execution of the remaining Gandillons the strange wolf killings in the area stopped and were never reported again.

Giza Death Star

The pyramids of the Giza plateau have long been a hot topic of debate for scientists and scholars alike. Their origins have constantly come under question as to their actual date, method and purpose of construction. But, there is one theory about their purpose that seems to create a great deal of controversy. That is whether or not they were originally designed and built as a power generator or a powerful weapon of mass destruction.

One of the largest proponents of the Giza Death Star theory is Joseph Ferrell, who hypothesizes that the nuclear energy of the hydrogen plasma inside the Great Pyramid was coupled to a superluminal "pilot wave" along with an acoustic and electromagnetic energy that was guided using harmonic interferometry to a given target. What resulted was a thermonuclear and nuclear reaction that caused the complete destruction of the target. Ferrell's theories are not so far-fetched, as there are actually legends from ancient China that talk of a great weapon that was called the "yin-yang mirror."

Possible evidence that a nuclear event did occur in the region at one time does exist. During the first atomic bomb tests in the New Mexico desert, the sand in the area was immediately fused into a green glass. According to the magazine *Free World*, archaeologists digging in the ancient Euphrates Valley of Egypt have actually uncovered a layer that shows an agrarian culture that is 8,000 years old and even older herdsman culture. Their digs have even uncovered evidence of cultures dating back to those of cavemen, but it is their most recent find that is the most shocking because in the oldest layer they found a layer of green glass identical to that found in the desert of New Mexico following the testing of the atomic bomb. This would seem to indicate that during that period a nuclear event of some type did occur in that region.

One question that has never been adequately answered is what happed to the king's body that was supposed to be in the king's chamber. The official version is that it was removed long before the tomb was officially opened by grave robbers, but the truth is that the size of the stone casket in the chamber is actually too small to hold an adult human body. In fact its actual dimensions match those of the Ark of the Covenant exactly. What makes this connection so intriguing is the fact that Moses was originally from Egypt and was trained in the methods of its priests. It would not be a long stretch to question if what he had the Israelites build in the desert was actually a copy of the power device that was once in the Great Pyramid.

Giants in the Desert of California

Located in the California desert are many mysterious places, but there is one just outside the small southern California town of Blythe that has many wondering who made the mysterious human and animal etchings into the desert surface. The etchings are enormous and there is no trace of the people who made them or any explanation as to why they made them.

Numbering at a half a dozen, the drawings are obviously human and animal figures, but their actual meaning is unknown. In order to see the enormous etchings one has to view them from the air, indicating that when they were drawn, they were not intended to be seen by anyone living on the ground. The figures are so large that one of the largest is 171 feet long making it impossible to view from the ground with the naked eye. They were first discovered in the 1930's, but it was not until 1952 that they were investigated by archaeologists who were unable to come to any conclusions as to their origins or purpose. They remain an unsolved mystery to this day and scientists have yet to discover any evidence that would offer any clues as to their existence.

Golem of Prague

Typically a creature of myth and legend, the Golem was created by a sorcerer from dirt and stone. In 1580, the legend may have become fact as a Jewish sorcerer in the town of Prague allegedly was given the magick formula to bring life to a man made of dirt. Rabbi Judah took the formula that he claimed was given to him by God and brought to life a violent creature of incredible strength that he kept hidden in his attic at the main synagogue in Prague.

Because the Golem was said to be immortal, it could not be destroyed and would have still been alive during World War II when it is rumored that it was transferred to Warsaw, Poland to fight the Nazi oppression of the Jews. According to accounts from occupation troops, there were several deaths that were attributed to a strange creature in Warsaw at the time.

Descriptions of the Golem vary, but the basic standard seems to be that it is the size of an average man, but with a lifeless face. The creature is said to lack the ability of speech and have arms that are longer and more muscular than that of a typical human male. Its skin is grey and its eyes are narrow slits giving one a sense of sheer terror. Lacking a soul and possessing an endless lifespan, the creature would still be alive today, if indeed the stories are true regarding its use in WWII. The story that it was returned to Prague would also be true and that is where it would still be today, alive and as pissed off as ever hidden away in the attic of the synagogue at Altneuschule waiting to be called back into duty once again.

H

Hampton Court Palace

Hampton Court Palace is located in Surrey, England and upstream of Central London on the River Thames. It is open to the public as a major tourist attraction and an estimated 55 million people have visited it.

Built in the 14th century and rebuilt by Thomas Wolsey, the Archbishop of York and Chief Minister to Henry VIII, it was eventually taken over by Henry VIII as a royal residence after Wolsey fell from his favor.

Much of Hampton Court Palace is designed in a classical Italian style, although some parts of it were made over into the Tudor style once Henry VIII took over. Henry VIII added the Great Hall which was the last medieval Great Hall built for the English monarchy and the Royal Tennis Court, which is still in use to this day.

With each succeeding royalty, Hampton Court was renovated many times until it ceased to be a royal residence and opened as a public place by Queen Victoria. It currently houses many works of art and furnishings. It also has a world-famous maze.

So it is not surprising, considering its age and history, that Hampton Court Palace is haunted. Most of the hauntings apparently happened around Henry VIII's time, although about over 30 apparitions have been reported from all ages. The main reports have consisted of:

- Henry VIII's 3rd wife, Jane Seymour, who gave birth to his son the future King Edward VI and died twelve days later, has been seen around the staircase in the Palace

- Henry VIII's 5th wife, Catherine Howard, has been seen, dressed in white, running down the Haunted Gallery with fear on her face and screaming for mercy.
- A ringed hand of a woman knocking on the door has been reported. When a witness drew the ring, it matched the ring worn by Catherine Howard
- A door outside Henry VIII's private chapel has been allegedly the cause of several women tourists fainting (it was the same door that Catherine Howard was knocking on begging for mercy, when under house arrest for adultery)
- Cold spots
- Edward VI's nurse, Sibell Penn still continues her visits

On December 19, 2003, as reported by the Associated Press, a closed-circuit security camera at Hampton Court had picked up what appeared to be the ghostly figure of a man dressed in robes, one arm reaching out for the door handle. A security guard said that the face did not look human, and a female palace visitor also reported possibly seeing a ghost in that area as well. It was suggested that it was the ghost of Archbishop Wolsey.

The Hampton Court Palace staff were perturbed enough to consult a psychologist, Dr. Richard Wiseman, who conducted an investigation there for four nights using video cameras, pressure gauges, EMF meters and a thermal camera. His findings were inconclusive, however.

Hell's Hum

Beginning in the 1990's, residents of the small New

Mexico town of Taos began to experience a strange noise that seemed to be coming from the ground beneath their feet. Some of the residents even paid visits to their doctors as a result of the constant ringing. At first doctors attributed the hum to what is medically known as tinnitus (a chronic ringing in the ears), but as time passed and the number of reported cases began to increase there seemed to be more to the picture. Eventually the residents of Taos began to start to also complain of headaches, insomnia and anxiety. At one point the events become so wide spread that they made front page news and scientist began to look into a possible underlying cause for the strange noise and physical side effects.

Scientists were actually able to measure and record the strange hum and concluded that it was related to ELF (Extreme Low Frequency) waves, which is a band of radio frequencies that range from 3 to 300 Hz. The United States Navy has been using ELF waves very successfully for many years to communicate with submarines while submerged. Because of the electrical conductivity of salt water, ELF waves are able to travel at great range and depth without the risk of being detected by surface radio methods. In order for ELF to be used on the surface, it would require an extremely large antenna, but in a salt water environment it requires very little.

The strange hum was not only heard in New Mexico, but was also heard in Northern California where it has, and continues to be, heard by thousands of residents from across the region. Whether military or electromagnetic from within the Earth, it is clear that the physical and mental effects on humans living in the range of the hum are being affected in a negative and inexplicable way.

I

Interstate 4 Death Zone

While many small towns try to lay claim to one of the most infamous titles in the country, there is only one that actually lives up to its name as the Interstate 4 Death Zone. It is a small one quarter mile patch of interstate that runs half way between Daytona and Orlando, Florida. This piece of gravel and tar has become the number one stretch of highway in the United States for accidents. Since its opening there have been between 1,048 to 1,740 automobile accidents on the bridge that runs across the St. Johns River in Seminole County.

The fact that the there is an unusually high number of accidents on the stretch of highway does not make it a mystery, but rather the history behind its construction and what may lay beneath the asphalt. During the 1880's the entire area was nothing but wilderness that was owned by Henry Sanford the head the Florida Land and Colonization Company. Sanford had the land divided into ten parcels in and attempt to try to establish a Roman Catholic community named Saint Joseph's Colony. Sanford believed that by using a religious front he could unload his otherwise worthless real estate quickly to devout believers in the faith.

To help pull off his scheme, he enlisted the services of a priest named Felix Swembergh to oversee the operation. In the beginning there were only four families that bought into Sanford's concept and by 1887 there was a sudden outbreak of yellow fever in the area that completely killed four members of one of the original families. At the time the priest, Father Swembergh, was out of town and had succumbed to the fever himself. The remaining survivors feared that the illness was airborne and immediately buried the bodies without having given them the last rites in accordance with their beliefs.

The sudden onset of yellow fever soon passed and the Catholic colony eventually became the town of Lake Monroe by 1890. Some of the land was cleared for farming, but there was a tiny cemetery that was left untouched where the bodies of the original victims of the fever lay buried. In 1905, the land changed hands again and was bought by Albert Hawkins. By the time he had purchased the land, the names of the dead had long since been eroded from the four tiny wooden grave markers. No one had any idea who the graves belonged to but the land owner, Albert Hawkins, held respect for the dead by telling those that leased his land to leave the small cemetery alone.

Unfortunately, it was when one of Mr. Hawkins' tenants decided to ignore the warning that the entire series of strange events began to occur. A tenant farmer decided to try to move a fence that marked the area of the graves and that same evening his home burned to the ground. But the tenant was not the only victim of a strange fire because when Mr. Hawkins chose to follow suit and tried to remove the fence his own home burned to the ground.

In 1959, the entire stretch of land was eventually purchased by the government as part of the path for the Interstate 4 highway. During the survey of the road, the graves were noted and marked for relocation in accordance with law, but due to a strange turn of events, the bodies were never moved. When the construction process began, the dirt was brought in as fill and ended up being dumped right on top of the small cemetery. Ironically, it was at that same time that Hurricane Donna hit Florida and passed directly over the area. Accounts have the actual eye of the hurricane passing directly over the grave site at exactly midnight on September 10, 1960.

Time passed and rebuilding went on. The interstate was eventually built and opened, but on its opening day, a tractor trailer mysteriously lost control and jackknifed directly above the graves. To date, the number of accidents continues to increase and the actual existence of the graves remains in question, but it cannot be denied that the location does seem to have a habit of inviting tragedy.

J

Jack the Ripper

No book of mysteries would be complete without including a piece on the only documented case of a successful serial killer. That is right, a serial killer that still remains unidentified to this day. His horrors have become legendary and his identity narrowed down, but not singled out long after his or her normal lifespan. While the identity of the illusive murderer remains a mystery, there are many questions as to why this was the only individual to ever have successfully taken the lives of fifteen living breathing human beings and never have been identified, much less brought to justice.

A faceless death dealer that once walked the streets of the poverty stricken streets of the Whitechapel district of London, this still remains one of the greatest mysteries of all times. While there were a number of murders in the area at the time that have been attributed to the elusive devil on Earth, the reality is that only about fifteen can actually be attributed to Jack the Ripper. The terror began with the murder of Mary Ann Nichols on August 31, 1888 and lasted for nine weeks ending in the brutal and needless slashing of Mary Kelly who was slaughtered in the same horrifying fashion as the previous fourteen victims of the sick and twisted soul.

The earlier slayings were some of the more crude and repulsive, as it seems that the killer was primarily concerned with being caught, rather than with precision. As an example it was during "his" attack of Long Liz that he was interrupted by the driver of a pony cart who found the woman lying in street and tried to lift her head to keep the blood from spilling from her throat. His efforts proved futile and the poor woman became another victim of the faceless killer. But following that night, Jack the Ripper began to pay more attention to detail and allow for an environment that allowed "him" to take the time to actually remove organs from the victims, something that was not normal at the time, but does have a sick and twisted place in the modern dark world of underground organ transplants.

Yes, there actually is an underground trade in illegally harvested human organs today. I have spoken with Dr. Tess Garrettson, M.D., a medical doctor and author, who has written many stories about horrifying tales of organ theft. But, that was not now and there was no need to take organs, or was there? One of the primary suspects in the Ripper case was a surgeon. There are actually three doctors that were considered as suspects in the case. At the time of the murders there was still a shortage of medical specimens available to science and it would not have been unreasonable to link a harvesting doctor to the crimes. Of the three, none were actually native to England and were Thomas N. Cream of America, Michael Ostrogg of Russia and Alexander Pedachenko, also of Russia. All had aliases and all had fraudulent and criminal offences that led police to suspect they might have been involved because they were all in the area at the time. Of the three, only Cream had actually been arrested for poisoning a prostitute and habitually writing to police, giving false names and crimes. Ostrogg also had several aliases, but most of his offences involved fraud and theft. The last, Pedachenko, also had numerous aliases and was considered a lunatic by authorities and was trained as a "barber's surgeon."

Doctors are not the only suspects in the crime. One suspect was John Pizer, a shoemaker and a Jew who happened to meet the public prejudice at the time. He had a stabbing conviction against him at the time and had a reputation for hating prostitutes. Unfortunately for Pizer, his appearance closely matched that of a drawing that had been circulated by authorities. The press immediately picked up on the connection and made it a point to publicize Pizer's "cruel sardonic look." The problem that authorities ran into was that in one of the messages that the Ripper sent to them he clearly stated:

> "*I'm not a butcher; I'm not a Yid,*
> *Nor yet a foreign skipper;*
> *But I am your own true loving friend*
> *---Yours truly, Jack the Ripper."*

This clearly indicated the killer was not any of the suspects mentioned above, but it is the line "But I am your own true loving friend" that is the dead giveaway. Why say this to the police? It was someone they knew, working with them, one of their own or someone that they answered to. The most popular suspect for this role is none other than a member of the royal family, Albert Victor, the Duke of Clarence. The needless murders stopped as suddenly as they began. The connection between the murders as Whitechapel and Albert Victor, "Prince Eddy" as he was known, was not made until 1962 when it was talked about in the work of Philippe Julien, author of Edouarda VII, which first published the allegations the then next in line to the throne may have been the infamous "Jack the Ripper."

Jersey Devil

There was a time on this planet when strange beasts once claimed the skies, but that time has passed and since there have been strange reports of a creature that seems to bring with it a great fear. The creature is said to roam the Pinelands of New Jersey and the surrounding areas. Its presence has been noted in public and paranormal records for the past 260 years. To date there have been more than 2,000 witnesses in the twentieth century alone. It has created terror in the hearts and minds of all who see it and the very sight of the creature itself still leaves eyewitnesses searching their souls for salvation.

Known as the Jersey Devil, it seems to have originated in folklore, but eventually became a part of unexplained history. There are many different versions about the actual origins of the Jersey Devil, but the fact remains that its presence is still felt and noticed today. A popular story of the origins begins with a Leeds Point, NJ resident named Mrs. Shrouds who did not want to have another child and if she did she said it would be the "Devil." She may have gotten her wish because when her unexpected child was born, it was disfigured and she immediately cast it out as a "Devil."

That is the basic story of the Jersey Devil, but the reality is probably far simpler. When Mrs. Shroud gave birth hoping for a "Devil," she was probably living in poverty conditions and her child most likely suffered from a birth defect when she cast it out. Tragically, it more than likely did not live, but there are actual accounts of flying birds and reptiles across North America that may account for the strange sightings in a more realistic manner.

There are actually now real legitimate records that document the story prior to the early 19th century when there were reports by Commodore Stephen Decatur and even Joseph Bonaparte, the former King of Spain and brother of Napoleon. By 1903, the story of the Jersey Devil had become so popular, and sightings on the increase, that Charles Skinner, the author of

American Myths and Legends, wrote that the sightings had run their course and would begin to decline until nobody heard anything else about them. That seemed to be the case for six years until January of 1909 when the elusive devil began to leave his footprints all over the South Jersey and Philadelphia. During the period in 1909, between January 16 and 23, the creature was seen by 100 people, the largest sighting ever.

There are many descriptions of the creature over the years, but the basic characteristics remained the same until recently. It was first described as about three feet high with the head of a collie and the face of a horse. It had a long neck and wings about two feet long with legs like a crane ending in a horse's hooves. Today that description has grown to six feet in size with an owl like face and red eyes. Regardless, there is a phenomenon occurring that does need to be investigated. There is obviously a creature in the remote regions of New Jersey that is currently unknown to science and extremely limited in number. Putting aside myth and pursuing actual investigation is the only way to determine whether or not there is a Devil in the dark woods New Jersey.

K

Kennedy Assassination

The thirty-fifth President of the United States of America, John Fitzgerald Kennedy, was riding in his motorcade through Dealey Plaza in Dallas, Texas on November 22, 1963 when gun shots rang out. The President was hit and pronounced dead less than an hour later. A day, which continues to live in the annals of American tragedies, it is also a day that spawned a controversial mystery that continues to this day.

Arrested for the shooting was Lee Harvey Oswald, who is still named as the official lone gunman in the assassination. The determination that Oswald acted alone was made by the Warren Commission, a commission set up to investigate the shooting and determine if Oswald had indeed acted alone or if there was a conspiracy in place to assassinate the President. The commission included Earl Warren, Chief Justice; Senators Richard B. Russell and John Cooper; U.S. Representatives Hale Boggs and Gerald R. Ford; and Allen W. Dulles, the former director of the Central Intelligence Agency.

The commission presented their final conclusion less than a year after the shooting in September of 1964 when they stated that there were three shots and all three shots had been fired by Lee Harvey Oswald from the sixth floor window of the Texas School Book Depository. The commission further concluded that no conspiracy had been involved in President's death. Unfortunately, their conclusion ended up being filled with too many holes.

The first problem arose when the commission claimed that a single bullet passed through President

Kennedy's body and continued on through until it struck Governor Connally, who was in the front seat of the open convertible they were all riding in. This shot is now known as the "magic bullet" because of angle that it would have had to be traveling at to hit both the President and the Governor where they were struck. This forensic determination simply does not add up. Then, a second shot from Oswald's rifle hit the President in the head, which was the fatal shot. After the first two shots were fired, the commission claims a third shot was fired, but missed. Oddly enough, all three shots that the commission claimed were fired by Oswald, would have had to be fired in an automatic three round burst. Oswald had used a single shot bolt action rifle, making it impossible for all three shots to have been fired from his rifle in that short a period of time.

Adding to the controversy is the testimony of former President Gerald Ford who was one of the actual participants in the Warren Commission. On July 3, 1997 he admitted that while working for the Warren Commission that he altered the documents to read that the bullet which hit Kennedy and then Connally had entered the President's body at the neck and not in his back where it actually struck. This change allowed the commission's report to seem valid by making the "magic bullet" theory very possible and eliminating the need to explain a sudden change in the bullet's direction. Ford never showed remorse for his admitted part in the cover-up and felt that this was only an attempt to be more precise. Calling altering the evidence being precise is like calling a bold faced lie the truth. But, then again, we are talking about a politician. The facts as they stand are in contrast with the findings of the Warren Commission and the public will likely never know the truth due to the level of possible government involvement in a conspiracy and cover-up.

Knights Templar

Often thought to be the original Christian order of Knights, there are actually orders that are older. The oldest order is the Knights of Saint John of Jerusalem which were also known as the Knights Hospitallers. It was around 1117 that the Knights Templar was founded by two French knights by the names of Hugues de Payens and Geoffrey of Saint-Omer. The pair had witnessed the hardships and victimization of Christian pilgrims on their way to the holy city of Jerusalem and was determined to do something to protect the weary and defenseless pilgrims.

When the pair set out on their mission to protect the innocent they had only one horse between them, but quickly gained a reputation for defending pilgrims on their way to Jerusalem. They were eventually joined by seven more men who chose to follow the pair's code of honor and defend the innocent. They quickly became known as the "Poor Soldiers of the Holy City" and chose to live a life of poverty for themselves and service to others. Word of their valor eventually reached the king of Jerusalem, Baldwin I, who granted the poor knights the privilege of staying in the Temple of Solomon. Because of their new home, they soon became known by the name we know them as today, the Knights Templar.

This is where the tale of the order of the Knights Templar takes a strange turn. As time passed, the group began to grow in numbers both in Europe and in Jerusalem. Oddly, the group was able to establish one of the first banking systems in history by taking money from pilgrims in Europe and then giving it back to them once they arrived in Jerusalem. Since they could not charge for this service because of their vow of poverty they began to take a form of interest on it. The Knights rapidly grew in wealth and began to buy property back home in Europe. The question that began to arise was where did the poor Knights get the money to start their banking system in the first place? In order for the Knights to give the first pilgrims that participated in their system their money back, they had to have money to give them when they got to Jerusalem. Where did that money come from if they had all taken vows of poverty?

Many suspected then, and now, that the sudden increase in wealth for the Knights came from discovering religious relics within the Temple they lived in. Some even claim that they actually uncovered the secret location under the Temple of the Ark of the Covenant. It is more likely that if they did discover anything, it was religious relics that would have been worth a fortune back in Europe during the era. This would have allowed the Knights to obtain the monetary backing necessary to begin their banking system.

Eventually, their wealth had grown and their seat of military power had fallen in the hands of the sultan Saladin. The surviving Knights returned to Europe, but the French lords, dukes and princes became envious of their wealth and angry over the fact that they were exempt from the high taxes that everyone else had to pay. The social and political elite began to raise charges of heretical practices by the group while they were in Jerusalem. Eventually King Philip IV would regain his political power in the region and begin to view the Knights as a potential threat to that power, the very same power that the Knights helped give him. King Philip decided to eliminate the threat and on the night of October 13, 1307, with support from the pope, sent his troops to every Templar castle in the region to round up the Knights. Nine hundred Knights were captured, imprisoned, and tortured. Thirty-six died while being tortured and some confessed to heresy to save them the pain of further torture.

On May 10, 1310, a grand council was held in Paris to review the confessions of the Templars, but during that time 54 of them had recanted their confessions and swore that they still remained true to their vows. Three days later, they were ordered burned at the stake by King Philip. As the last Grand Master of the Knights Templar, Jacques de Molay, stood burning at the stake in front of Notre Dame in 1314, he used his final breath to invite the Pope and King Philip to join him at heaven's gate.

Kongomato

Throughout history there have been reports from all over the world of large strange flying creatures, but the fossil record tells us that creatures that closely match some of these descriptions actually existed. About 65 million years ago, a simple blink of an eye in terms of Earth's history, existed a group of flying Dinosaurs known as Pterosaurs.

Pterosaurs appeared in the fossil record around the Jurassic period and survived well into the Cretaceous period. The majority of the fossils found for these flying reptiles have been located in marine deposits which indicate that they would have had a diet high in fish proteins. They were a very strange mix of various modern species. They had the beak and bones of a bird, but lacked feathers. Their wings were composed of a membrane that was stretched out across an elongated fourth finger very much like that of a bat. But they were cold blooded reptiles that had a limited ability to regulate their body temperature very much like turtles. The need to be able to regulate their body temperature, even to a limited ability, would have been essential to their survival and their need to maintain flight for long periods of time.

Unlike many of the modern movies that depict these creatures, the majority of them were actually much smaller than the media portrays them. They ranged in average size from that of a sparrow to the size of an eagle. There were some species that did grow larger, such as the pteranodon which had an average wingspan of 27 feet and the colossal quetzalcoatlus which had an average wingspan of 50 feet, but these species were rare and far fewer fossils of them have been found.

At this point you may be asking yourself, "What do fossils have to do with a modern monster?"

The answer is simple in that there is a very real possibility that since Pterosaurs did have a limited ability to regulate their body temperature and they were not limited to one geographic location thanks to their ability to fly, they may have actually survived like some of the other species. Their diet of fish would mean that they could survive just about anywhere with a warm climate. It is not unreasonable to hypothesize that a localized population of Pterosaurs still exists in the less populated regions of the Africa.

The first modern report of such a creature came in 1923 while Frank Melland was working in Zambia. He began to hear strange stories about a mysterious flying creature that the natives called the Kongamoto, which translates into "overwhelmer of boats." The creature lived in the Jiundi swamps in the Mwinilunga District of western Zambia, along the borders of Congo and Angola. The native people were so fearful of the creatures that they often carried charms that they called "muchi wa Kongamato" to protect them when crossing certain rivers in the region that were known to be frequented by the beasts.

The local natives of the region often recognize pictures of Pterosaurs as the Kongamato when shown pictures. They also claim that the beasts are extremely dangerous and often attack their boats. Attempts to track down these mysterious creatures have yet to yield any successful results, but researchers continue their efforts in hopes of discovering the truth behind these mysterious creatures' existence one day soon. In the meantime the local natives continue to keep one eye on the skies overhead while on the rivers of the region.

L

Leap Castle

Located in Offaly County about four miles north of Roscrea, Leap Castle was built in approximately 1250 in order to guard the pass from Slieve Bloom into Munster. The original Gaelic name for it was *Leím Uí Bhanáin* meaning "Leap of the O'Bannons."

The O'Bannon family were actually subject to the ruling O'Carroll clan who used Leap as its principal ruling seat, but then took it over to reside there themselves as it was practically impossible to attack. The records of the Annals of the Four Masters reflect that the Earl of Kildare, Gerald FitzGerald tried to seize it in 1513, but was unsuccessful. However, three years later, he attacked the castle again and managed to destroy a part of it.

Chief Mulrooney O'Connell had two sons, the one-eyed Tadhg and another who was a priest. When the Chief died, there was a fight over the leadership within the family. The O'Connell priest was holding mass in the castle chapel when Tadhg burst in and slew him with an ax or a sword. To this day the chapel is called the "Bloody Chapel." Right after the murder of his brother, Tadhg invited certain members of the clan to a lavish banquet. Just as they seated themselves, Tadhg had his servants murder them, thus ensuring that the leadership was his alone.

Many other people were also imprisoned, tortured and executed in the castle. The dungeon was infamous in its day for that reason with its oubliette in which a corpse would be dumped down a drop door. When workers were cleaning it out in the 1900's, they had to have three cartloads of bones found at the bottom of the oubliette carried away.

Castle Leap eventually passed into the hands of a Darby who married an O'Connell daughter in 1659 and remained in the family until 1922, in which the castle was burned and looted during the Irish civil war. A Jonathan Charles Darby inherited the castle in 1880 and it was his wife, Mildred Darby who held séances at the castle and dabbled with magic.

It is not surprising that Leap Castle acquired a reputation for being haunted even prior to Mildred Darby's occult work, but she may have made matters worse by calling up something that is known as the "Elemental." In 1909, she wrote an article for the *Journal Occult Review* in which she tells the story of her experience. "I was standing in the Gallery looking down at the main floor, when I felt somebody put a hand on my shoulder. The thing was about the size of a sheep. Thin gaunting shadowy…its face was human, to be more accurate inhuman. Its lust in its eyes which seemed half decomposed in black cavities stared into mine. The horrible smell one hundred times intensified came up into my face, giving me a deadly nausea. It was the smell of a decomposing corpse."

Eventually the castle was sold to an Australian, then to the current owners, the Ryans, who still live there. Sean Ryan had two freak accidents in which he broke a kneecap and then soon afterwards his ankle when doing renovations on the castle, but stoutly claimed that he and his family "would be happy to share the castle with the spirits as long as there are no more occurrences."

Reports of hauntings include:

- The elemental who is malevolent, terrifying and unpredictable and usually accompanied by a foul smell as described by Mildred Darby.

- The ghost of the priest who was killed in the Bloody Chapel by his brother.
- A lady in red, sometimes carrying a dagger.
- A window in the Bloody Chapel which would suddenly light up as though Mass was being performed when Leap Castle was empty for seventy years.
- A ghostly man seated in a chair by a downstairs fireplace.

Leap Castle has been profiled in several television shows, most notably LivingTV's *Most Haunted* and SciFi's *Ghost Hunters*. According to a website on castles in Ireland, the castle is open year-round but there are no accommodations, so if you are brave enough, it may be worth a visit should you be in the area!

Leprechaun

A leprechaun is considered to be in a class with the "faerie folk" in Ireland in that it is typically described as a type of a male faerie who is often described as a little old man with a beard and practices shoemaking. The typical appearance of a leprechaun is that of a redhead wearing all green with a black top hat, but that has been attributed to being an American invention for commercial purposes. Samuel Lover wrote in 1831 that a leprechaun is *"quite a beau in his dress notwithstanding, for he wears a red square cut coat, richly laced with gold, and inexpressible of the same, cocked hat, shoes and buckles."*

The term leprechaun comes from various meanings in the old Irish language such as *Leipreachán* (pigmy or sprite) or *luchorpán* (pigmy, an aqueous sprite, small-bodied, half-bodied). The Oxford English Dictionary also has an alternative word, *leath bhrógan* meaning shoemaker.

Interestingly enough, leprechauns do not rate their own folk tales, but instead appear in stories centered on human heroes. They are generally described as harmless, solitary and live in remote locations, although some can be nasty and mischievous. They are also described as very well spoken and could make good conversation.

The most popular view of leprechauns is that they are wealthy and like to hide their treasures (left by the Danes when they invaded Ireland) in secret locations which could only be revealed if a person could catch them or find their pot of gold at the end of a rainbow. This is the reason the leprechauns avoid all contact with humans who they consider as foolish and greedy creatures.

Ley Lines

"Ley lines" or straight lines in alignment stretching across the landscape, was first documented in a talk titled "Boundaries and Landmarks" presented to the British Archaeological Society by William Henry Black in 1870. In his talk, he stated "Monuments exist marking grand geometrical lines which cover the whole of Western Europe."

However, it was the better known Alfred Watkins, a Herefordshire businessman and an amateur archaeologist, who documented his observations in a book in 1925 *The Old Straight Track*:

Alfred Watkins was riding near some hills when he noticed many of the footpaths seemed to connect to one hilltop to another in a straight line. He was studying a map when he saw "in a flash" a whole pattern of lines in alignment stretching across the landscape. He believed that ancient Britain, when more densely covered in forests, had been crisscrossed by a network of straight-line trading routes, with the prominent landmarks being used as navigation points.

However, archaeologists refused to accept his ideas particularly due to the fact the causes of the straight line alignments are disputed, even though in 2004 John Bruno Hare wrote that Watkins never attributed the ley lines to the supernatural. Skeptics to this day think that ley lines do not exist and the straight lines are purely coincidental. They also point out that straight lines are impossible for ideal roads, especially since if the travelers go up and down hills and mountains or cross rivers where there are no bridges.

Another interpretation due to a new and major aspect of archaeological study called archaeogeodesy, ley lines could be the product of prehistoric surveying, property markings or commonly travelled pathways and they have been documented by archaeologists as it is reasonable to expect humans to build these types of lines.

An example of the ancient cultures using straight lines across the landscape is reflected in the Nasca lines in South America. These lengthy lines often are directed towards the mountain peaks and especially in Mexico, connect the pyramids.

Most popular interpretation, especially among the New Age people, is that the intersecting ley lines give off a special psychic or mystical energy. The occultist Dion Fortune in *The Goat-Foot God* written in 1936, was the author who invented the idea that the ley lines were "lines of power" linking prehistoric sites. Later on, it was suggested that ley lines could be found by dowsing rods as they were part of the cosmic energy in the Earth, and it is documented that the Chinese, Greeks, Irish and Scottish men built their temples where the earth forces were very powerful.

One of the most visible and interesting sites in connection with the ley lines is located at Glastonbury Tor. According to the Glastonbury Tor website:

"The Michael and Mary lines are especially powerful. They connect major sacred sites throughout the South West and beyond. But it's only on the Tor that their energies combine. In a harmonious dance of earth patterns, the lines move ever closer as they approach the summit. At the top, they merge and unite. Perhaps this is what makes it easy for so many other kinds of opposites to harmoniously come together on the Tor."

The Michael line is called that because most of the churches on it are dedicated to St. Michael, who was the Christian version of the protective male deity originally associated with this line. In the same way, St. Mary churches delineate the Mary line and replaced older shrines to a nurturing and gentle earth mother. The male and female nature of the two lines was thus preserved and continued by the Christian interpretation. When they flow down from the Tor again, the lines then pass through the other major Glastonbury sites – Chalice Well, the Abbey and Wearyall Hill. Their energy may be an important source of the strong mystical element that's been associated with these places for many hundreds of years."

Apart from their connection with sacred sites, these lines are also associated with strange lights, and other unexplained phenomena. Over the years, a substantial number of credible witnesses have seen balls of light around the Tor.... Whatever these lights are, they seem connected in some way with the powerful energies of sacred sites and earth meridians."

In the 1960's, ley lines also became linked with UFO sightings because of their electrical and magnetic forces attracting the UFOs. It is also suggested by parapsychologists that intersecting ley lines could be related to hauntings, particularly in poltergeist cases.

M

Mason Inn House

Built in 1846, the Mason House Inn is located in historic Bentonsport, Iowa (southeast of the city of Des Moines). Bentonsport, which has the distinction of being one of the first settlements in Iowa, is located right on the Des Moines River. The Mormon craftsmen coming from Nauvoo, Illinois (they were on their way to Salt Lake City, Utah and stopped in Bentonsport to work and gather supplies) were the builders of this lovely place to serve as a hotel for weary steamboat travelers.

It was originally known as the Ashland Hotel before being purchased by Lewis Mason and his wife Nancy. The name was changed to Phoenix House after their purchase, but the townspeople referred to it as the Mason House and the name has stuck to this day. It was Nancy Mason who started the tradition of a cookie jar in every room, which is carried on even to this day by the current innkeepers!

The Mason House was used as a "holding hospital" during the Civil War for injured soldiers who were waiting for the train or boats to take them to the hospital in Keokuk. It was also the site of an Underground Railroad.

The Mason family owned the house for 99 years, then it was sold to Herbert and Burretta Redhead who ran the inn as a bed and breakfast as well as a museum for 33 years. Bill and Sheral McDermet purchased the hotel in 1989 and did a lot of work on it until they sold it in 2001 to Chuck and Joy Hanson, who are the current owners of the Mason House Inn. Mason House Inn still retains much of its original furnishings from the Mason family.

With its 162 years of existence, it should come as no surprise that there have been many deaths in the Mason House Inn. Most of the Mason family members are reported to be still around as well as victims of several murders or the Civil War.

A partial list of the paranormal phenomenon throughout the whole place (<u>every</u> room is reported to have paranormal incidents) includes:

- Knocks on doors early in the morning
- Rattling doorknob in one of the bathrooms
- Opening and closing doors
- Footsteps
- Cold spots and breezes
- Sleeping people getting poked or ticked in their beds
- Several full-bodied apparitions, including a cat named Josephine
- Sound of children running around when there are none in the Mason House Inn
- Visible orbs
- Unexplained mists or fog
- Rearranged items such as silverware or people's belongings

According to the Hansons, the ghosts are friendly and won't bother you if you ask them to leave you alone! However, Room 7 (there are 8 rooms used for travelers in addition to the kitchen, dining room, parlor and the Hanson's private residence) is reported by some people to have a negative, heavy feeling as though something bad happened there.

Outside the Mason Inn House is a yard where there was an underground tunnel that collapsed, burying three slaves in it. Apparitions of the three slaves have been reported coming out of the ground where the tunnel used to be. Chuck Hanson is considering digging it up one of these days to see if there are still bodies buried there!

Across from the Mason Inn House is the Bentonsport Bridge. The figure of a man walking across the bridge is also reportedly seen by some people during the evening. Also across the road is the Greef General Store, where paranormal activity is also experienced. The Hansons, are excellent hosts and very knowledgeable about not only the Mason House Inn, but the town of Bentonsport and its sister town, Bonaparte, located about ten minutes away. See www.masonhouseinn.com for more information. If you ask, the Hansons will also gladly give you an entire rundown of the ghostly happenings at Mason Inn House. Joy Hanson has kept a journal since 2001, and the results are published in two volumes called *Ghostly Happenings at the Mason House Inn*, which you can purchase from her for a nominal fee.

Mothman

In 2002, a movie called *The Mothman Prophecies*, starring Richard Gere, Laura Linney and Debra Messing was released. Richard Gere played a journalist who goes to Point Pleasant, Virginia due to a tragic incident in his life and becomes involved with the town's sightings of a strange creature. This is based on true-life incidents in which residents of this Appalachian town reported seeing a tall, winged man-creature with large red eyes and moth-like wings.

The Mothman was a name invented by an Ohio

newspaper after people were reporting "Big Bird" sightings. The Mothman was first reported in November of 1966 when two young married couples from Point Pleasant, David and Linda Scarberry and Steve and Mary Mallette were driving late at night in the Scarberrys' car. They were driving by an abandoned WWII TNT factory when they saw two red lights by an old generator plant near the factory gate. The four young people stopped to take a look and discovered that the red lights were the glowing eyes of a large animal "shaped like a man, but bigger, maybe six and a half or seven feet tall, with big wings folded against its back." The now scared people drove off and the creature supposedly chased them at speeds more than 100 miles per hour. In driving away, they spotted a dead dog on the side of the road and noted its location. They reported the sighting to Deputy Millard Halstead, who knew these people all their lives and took them so seriously that he went out and checked the site, but found nothing.

A local building contractor by the name of Newell Partridge reported hearing a strange sound coming from a nearby hay barn and saw his hunting dog Bandit facing it. When Newell pointed his flashlight in that direction, he saw two red eyes and terrified, ran back to his house. Bandit disappeared and never was found again. It was assumed that the dead dog that the four couples saw may have been Bandit.

Over the next several months, sightings continued to be reported in the Point Pleasant area. In December of 1967, the Silver Bridge, an eye bar chain suspension bridge built in 1928 that connected Point Pleasant with Kanauga, Ohio over the Ohio River collapsed. The cause was due to a failure of a single eye bar in a suspension chain due to a manufacturing flaw, but people blamed the Mothman for the collapse of the bridge. The sightings of the Mothman apparently decreased after the collapse of the bridge in which 47 people died.

John Keel wrote *The Mothman Prophecies* (the 2002 movie was based on this book) in which he claims that there were other paranormal events related to the Mothman sightings, such as UFO activity, Men in Black encounters, poltergeist activity, Bigfoot, black panthers, animal and human mutilations as well as the Silver Bridge collapse.

Conversely, Loren Coleman wrote *Mothman and Other Curious Encounters* in which he only discusses it from a cryptozoological point of view, describing the possibility of an undiscovered giant bird which may account for the Mothman sightings. Other people have theorized that the creature may have been either a Sandhill crane, which has an average wingspan of 7 feet, can glide without flapping and has an unusual shriek, or an owl. The red eyes are said to be caused by the reflection of lights, such as a flashlight.

N

Native Americans and their Perspective on Ghosts/Spirits

In taking an in-depth look at the Native American cultures and their perspective on ghosts/spirits, while there were different Native American cultures with its distinct tribal identity, they all shared certain traits that included spirituality as the central foundation of tribal and personal life, a belief that everyone and everything is related (hence their deep respect for life and kinship to the land), which included the interrelation of the natural and supernatural.

The following concepts that the Native Americans had in common, although their expression differed:

- Existence of unseen powers or spirits.
- Interdependence of all forms of life in the universe.
- Form of worship that reinforces personal commitment to sources of life.
- Sacred traditions that teach morals and ethics.
- Trained practitioners who pass on sacred practices.
- A belief that humor is a necessary part of the sacred to remind us of our human weaknesses.

Interestingly, the "great spirits" are not the typical ghosts or demons that we are accustomed to thinking of today. These "great spirits" were considered to be the very spirits of nature herself – the sun and moon, the sky, the earth, the sea, trees, animals and mankind.

These were not worshipped so much as seen as an expression of the Creator or Great Spirit and therefore, must be treated with great respect, which explains offerings left by the Native Americans for them such as corn pollen or other precious materials and such practices as if there was dead wood on the ground for fire wood, they will not cut down a living tree (karma, or "do unto others as you would have them do unto you"). The American Thanksgiving tradition is actually based on the elaborate thanksgiving ceremonies that the Native Americans performed in giving thanks to the spirits.

While some tribes believed in the Creator or "Great Spirit" and trusted in the number of spirits that he sent, others believed that the best of their maidens and warriors went on to become spirit guides to keep their people on the right path. Some other tribes also perceived animal spirits as an important source of knowledge, strength and character. Rituals and ceremonies were also a very important process of contacting and honoring these spirits.

Native Americans considered all souls to be immortal and therefore, a fair exchange of human and animal souls were required. For example, if the warriors went to hunt animals, it was necessary for them to treat the mortal remains of the killed animals with honor and respect for that reason as the shaman (medicine man/woman) of that tribe would work out with the animal spirit in charge of particular hunted animals a "redistribution" of souls.

While in many tribes, the spirits of the dead were seen as helpers, there were a few tribes who regarded the returned spirits as bad luck in which they would appear to friends and family and beg them to join them in the afterlife. For that reason, some tribes buried their people as far away from their home villages as possible, which explain some of the islands across the river being used as their cemeteries so the spirits could not cross the river.

Overall, the Native Americans believed that a person strived to live well, with respect for others in order to live a full life and reach old age. Death was greatly respected in all Native American traditions because of its inevitability. It was not feared or seen as the end of life by most tribes as it was a natural part of life and a transition into the afterlife. The afterlife varied according to the beliefs of the different tribes.

Unfortunately, the arrival of the Europeans resulted in the loss of many of the traditional beliefs, although ironically, there were some similarities in the Native Americans' and Europeans' beliefs such as respect for people and the belief in the afterlife.

Nuckelavee

The most feared of all the elves, this Scottish creature is said to be a skinless amphibian like beast with a horse's body from the waist down. It is said that the beast brings diseases and ruins crops with its deadly breath. It is also know to suck the life right out of the living in an almost vampire-like manner.

The Nuckelavee has the nose of a pig and its head sways on its body as it trots along while crops wither as it passes by. Both humans and animals alike fall prey to in the wake of the droughts and plagues it leaves behind. It is said that the only protection or means to repel the foul creature is to carry a bottle of fresh water, which will allow you to escape its grasp before it can take your life force giving you time to hurt it with a pair of iron scissors. Or, if you are lucky enough to be near running water and may cross it so that the creature will be unable to follow.

O

Ogopogo

During hockey season, it is not uncommon to attend a game of the Kelowna Rockets and see a rather unusual-looking creature as the team's logo. This creature has allegedly lurked around the depths of Canada's lake Okanagan and been both the topic of fun and fear alike. Like its European cousin, the famous Loch Ness Monster, the creature in Lake Okanagan, or Ogopogo as it has affectionately become known, has been filmed and photographed many times during the 20th century. But there is a great misconception between Ogopogo and its Scottish cousin, Nessie. This misconception is the fact that while both claim a long history and existence prior to the twentieth century, it is actually Ogopogo that was first brought to the public's attention by the media back in 1926 while the Loch Ness Monster's first official media appearance would not be until 1933 as a result of the Spicer sighting.

Just like the Scottish creature, Ogopogo has a long history, but its history seems to be well rooted in native North American history. The Native North Americans that currently live in the area of the reservation that is located in the Okanagan Valley near the lake believe that the Ogopogo is not the friendly and loveable creature that the local tourist trade has come to depend on. Instead they not only claim to know exactly where the creature lives, but that it is to be feared and respected at a distance.

They call the lake creature *Shalish N'ha-a-tik* or "snake in the lake" and believe that its home is Rattlesnake Island near Squally Point. They would often report having found the remains of animals on the beach of the island that had been partially devoured by the creature of the lake. So terrified of Ogopogo were they that the Native Americans would not fish near Squally Point and when they were forced to cross the lake in bad weather they would always carry an animal to toss in the lake to distract the beast so they could cross safely. In fact, in 1860, a non Native American settler was leading a team of horses across the lake when he reported having several of them disappear under the water near Rattlesnake Island.

Out of Body Experiences

The term "Out of Body Experience" or OBE, the acronym that the phenomena has commonly come to be known as, was first coined by G.N.M. Tyrrell back in 1943. While Tyrrell was the first individual to bring public attention to the phenomena in the twentieth century, it has been around for much longer. There are Egyptian tomb paintings that appear to depict the "ba" or the "soul" hovering like a bird over the corps of the dead, indicating that the Ancient Egyptians may have had some belief or awareness of the phenomena.

Since Tyrrell's initial research began into the OBE phenomena it has taken on many other names, such as:

- Spirit Walking
- Astral Projection
- Autoscopy

Out of Body Experiences have been reported by many famous people such as Arthur Koestler, Virginia Woolf, and even Ernest Hemingway. In fact, over a quarter of all Americans report having had at least one

OBE experience during their lifetime. While the numbers and the historical facts would seem to indicate that there is something very real at work on the minds and bodies of humans, science has a very different answer.

OBEs occur in a wide range of individuals, both male and female from a wide range of ages, social economic and ethnic backgrounds. There seems to be no specific group that is predisposed to the phenomena. However, there seem to be a number of explanations that have been offered by scientists such as Dr. Michael Persinger who has experimented with a sensory deprivation helmet that directs electromagnetic waves at the temporal lobes of the brain in an attempt to simulate OBEs, to neurologists who have experimented with virtual reality devices and conducted research with psychotropic and psychedelic drugs in an attempt to induce OBEs.

The experience has also been reported to have been induced by a number of other methods. One method that has been practiced for centuries is visualization and meditation. This method is still popular today with most practitioners of magickal or mystical belief systems. This phenomenon has also been rarely reported as having occurred in some individuals during the BDSM extreme sexual practice known as mummification.

While there are still many more questions than answers and what appears to be the ability for the phenomena to spontaneously manifest on its own. It also seems to be possible for we as humans to have the ability to induce it in using a variety of methods, but whatever the means of induction there are experts on both sides of the coin that seem to agree on one thing, and that is whatever is accruing does have a very real effect on the minds and lives of the individuals that experience it.

P

Pike Place Market

Upon first glance, the Pike Place Market in Seattle, Washington, is not a place that you would think has ghosts. It is nationally recognized as America's premier farmers' market and has nearly 200 commercial businesses, 190 craftspeople, 120 farmers (who rent table space by the day) and 240 street performers and musicians. It also has 300 apartment units which are inhabited mostly by elderly people. The locals affectionately call it, "The Market," and attract 10 million visitors a year.

Pike Place Market has nine acres and has operated for over 100 years. It was founded on August 17, 1907 because a Seattle City Councilman by the name of Thomas Revelle proposed a public street market that would connect the farmers directly with the consumers who were fed up with paying middle-men high prices for produce. An example was the cost of onions which increased tenfold between 1906 and 1907. The first day the Market opened, there were eight farmers who brought their wagons and were quickly bombarded by 10,000 eager shoppers! By the end of 1907, the first Market building opened, with every space filled. There was a philosophy put in place where the customers would "Meet the Producer" directly, that still holds true to this day. To get more information, visit the Market's website at www.pikeplacemarket.org.

However, being around for over a hundred years, it's not surprising that the Market is allegedly haunted. The most famous reported ghost is that of a Native American princess, one of the daughters of Chief Sealth (which was Anglicized into Seattle, whom the city of Washington was named after). Princess Angelina lived in a small shack built on stilts surrounded by mudflats, where she dug clams for a living and sold them to customers on the site where the Market is today. A famous photographer, Edward S. Curtis, made friends with her and gave her one dollar for each photograph he took of her. She died sometime in May of 1896. Her ghost is usually described as an elderly woman wearing a shawl and shabby clothes or dressed in white, with bright blue eyes.

Market developer Arthur Goodwin and his uncle, Frank Goodwin, who was the principal investor, are also reported to appear in several locations throughout the market, particularly in the Goodwin Library. Other sightings include:

- A pole that is icy cold no matter how hot the day.
- An eerie lullaby that echoes throughout the Market (it is believed to be the ghost of a lady barber who worked there years ago and was famous for lulling her patrons to sleep with her singing so she could pick their pockets).
- Sightings of a dancing man who wears a double-breasted suit from World War II (Boeing Aircraft used to stage Saturday dances in one of the upstairs halls, now destroyed by a fire). Women who actually danced with him reported that he was unusual in that he was too light and too fast on his feet, with his hands not very substantial. When they compared notes, they concluded he was a ghost!
- In a store called the Bead Emporium, a little blonde boy ghost plays with beads by unraveling strings of beads, hiding them or throwing them at customers.
- A book-throwing ghost at Shakespeare Books.

For those that are interested in meeting the ghosts and other weird things of the Market, there is the Market Ghost Tour run by Mercedes Yaeger. Information can be found at www.seattleghost.com. Even if one isn't interested in hunting down these hauntings, the Market is well worth a visit for its shopping and colorful ambience!

Q

Queen Anne's (Boleyn) Ghost

Anne Boleyn was the second of Henry VIII's six wives and one of the most famous, for it was her marriage to the King of England that brought about a huge political and religious upheaval in England that was the beginning of the Church of England's break with Rome and under the control of the monarchy of England afterwards.

She was crowned Queen of England in June of 1533 and in September, gave birth to the future Queen Elizabeth I of England. By March 1536, Henry was paying court to his future wife, Jane Seymour, as he was very unhappy with Anne for failing to produce a male heir. To get Anne out of the way, he had her investigated for charges, including adultery, incest and high treason to the crown. On May 19, 1536, she was beheaded and it was remarked that she died very bravely, kneeling upright and saying her final prayers prior to the deadly stroke of the axe. She was buried in an unmarked grave in an arrow chest, but during renovations during the reign of Queen Victoria, her skeleton was identified and her grave marked in the marble floor of the Chapel of St. Peter ad Vincula. Historians have since stated the charges against her were fake and not to be believed.

After her death, all sorts of stories began to rise. She was believed to have a third nipple and a sixth finger on her left hand; that she had an aversion to church bells, witchery. She was also accused of attempts at poisoning, particularly Henry VIII's first wife Catherine of Aragon and her daughter, Mary Tudor. In spite of these negative allegations, Anne Boleyn was venerated as a martyr and the most influential and important queen consort, particularly due to her strong education, intelligence, wit and political acumen. She even wrote her own obituary in the Tower of London:

"Oh Death
Rock me asleep
Bring on my quiet rest
Let pass my very guiltless ghost
Out of my careful breast
Ring out the doleful knell
Let it sound
My death tell
For I must die."

Queen Anne's ghost seems to travel widely throughout various places, particularly on the anniversary of her death on May 19th. It is said that on that anniversary, she travels in a coach pulled by headless horses and driven by a headless horsemen to Blickling Hall in Norfolk (Blicking was where the Boleyn family was from). She is described as having her "dripping severed head in her lap." The coach disappears when it reaches the Hall, leaving the ghost of Anne to enter the Hall and to wander along the corridors until dawn

At Hever Castle in Kent, the seat of the Boleyn family and childhood home of Queen Anne, similar stories abound of her arrival in a black funeral coach drawn by six great black headless horses racing along the avenue to Hever Castle. Her ghost is said to appear around Christmastime and walking the bridge crossing the river to the castle grounds.

At Rochford Hall in Essex, the ghost of a headless woman in silks appears, attributed to Queen Anne as her father was Viscount Rochford before he became the Earl of Wiltshire.

In 1882 the *Spectre Stricken*, an excerpt from *Ghostly Visitors*, described the account of a Captain of the Guard, who saw a light burning in the locked Chapel Royal. He immediately got a ladder, looked through the window and saw a stately spectral procession led by Anne Boleyn, who was not beheaded. Even though her head was averted, the Captain recognized her elegant figure from the portraits of the Queen.

Most famous of the haunting are located at the Tower of London, the site of her death. In 1817, a sentry had a heart attack and died after meeting her ghost on a stairway. In 1864, another sentry was at his post near the Lieutenant's Lodgings when he challenged a white figure and drove his bayonet through it. He fainted when a "fiery flash ran through his weapon." He was court-martialled for being found asleep, but was not found guilty and acquitted when many witnesses came to describe seeing a headless ghost in the area. The best testimony came from an officer who had, from his room in the Bloody Tower, heard the challenge and looked outside, witnessing the whole scene. She also frightened another guard by walking straight into his bayonet in 1933 so that he fled screaming for help.

Queen Anne's ghost apparently goes from the Queen's House to the Chapel of Saint Peter ad Vincula where she walks down the aisle to her grave under the altar or walks the corridors of the White Tower. All these hauntings seem to bear out the theory of hauntings caused by a traumatic and/or unjust death.

R

Roanoke Island and the Lost Colony

One of the most enduring unsolved mysteries in early American history, Roanoke Island, located off of mainland North Carolina, certainly stands out as a place where 115 English settlers disappeared without a trace.

Roanoke Island was the brainstorm of Sir Walter Raleigh in the late 16th century in order to establish a permanent English settlement as part of a financial agreement or charter between Queen Elizabeth I and Raleigh. The agreement ensured riches from the New World and a base for raiding the Spanish settlements which were located in the southern part of the New World.

It was first discovered in 1584 by Philip Amadas and Arthur Barlowe, who were explorers sent to the area by Raleigh and they came back to England stating that Roanoke Island was the perfect place to settle in. A year later, Raleigh sent 100 men there under military captain Ralph Lane's supervision. Unfortunately, the first group did not work out due to arriving too late for the planting season and the fact that Lane alienated the neighboring Roanoke Indians by murdering their chief. The settlement was deserted when most of the men left with Sir Francis Drake on one of his stops from his raids, leaving behind a fort, which can still be seen today. Fifteen men remained behind, but when the second group came, no trace of them were ever found. They were assumed to be killed or according to the Croatan Indians (from the modern day Hatteras Island), they had sailed away.

The second group consisted of 117 colonists, led

by Governor John White, who was a good friend of Raleigh's. His daughter, Elizabeth Dare was pregnant when the group arrived on Roanoke Island, giving birth on August 18, 1587 to the first child born in America, Virginia Dare.

Governor White did his best to establish relations with the neighboring Indians, but the tribe whose chief was killed by Lane, refused to meet the new people. A colonist was killed when crabbing, so the remaining colonists begged White to return to England to explain their situation and to ask for help. He did so reluctantly, but was not able to return until around 1590, three years later due to the invasion of the Spanish Armada and lack of funds and seaworthy boats.

White actually landed on Roanoke Island the day of his granddaughter's third birthday on August 18, 1590, but found the settlement deserted and all the houses and fortifications dismantled, even though there were no signs of a battle. Only two skeletons were found. The only other clue they found was the word "Croatoan" carved into a fort post and "Cro" carved into a nearby tree. Before White left, he had arranged that if anything happened to the colony, someone was to carve a Maltese cross on a tree, but he found no such thing. They were not able to undertake a search and actually left the next day, with White never seeing his family again.

There were many theories that floated about as to the lost colony's fate, many of them implausible and even part of a hoax. The most popular theory was that the lost colony was assimilated in the neighboring Croatoan tribe. In the 1880's, a North Carolina resident named Hamilton MacMillan put forth the theory that actually seemed to make sense. He lived in Robeson County in southeastern North Carolina near a settlement of Pembroke Indians. Apparently the Pembroke Indians "spoke pure Anglo Saxon English, had the European features for fair eyes and light hair, and bore names of the lost colonists."

They also referred to their ancestors as coming from "Roanoke in Virginia" which was the original name that Raleigh and his peers had given Roanoke Island. Even though historians and archaeologists regularly check the sites on Roanoke Island, no one has ever been able to solve the mystery of Roanoke Island and the lost colony to this day.

S

Stone of Destiny

The Stone of Destiny is either the Scottish "Stone of Scone" or the Irish "*Lia Fáil*." Both of them have the common trait of being used as coronation stones of the ruling monarchs, although they differ in legends and looks.

The Stone of Scone has several legends reflecting its beginnings such as being the pillow stone of Jacob of the biblical fame, traveling altar of St. Columbia when on his missionary trips, or a coronation stone of the early Gaels when they lived in Ireland. It is an oblong block of red sandstone about 26 inches by 16 inches by 10.5 inches in size and weighing approximately 336 pounds, with iron rings at each end of the stone. When the stone was in Scone, it served as the seat of the Scottish monarchs beginning with Kenneth Mac Alpin, the first King of the Scots at around 847.

Another story is that Robert the Bruce actually gave a portion of the stone to Cormac McCarthy, king of Munster for his support at the battle of Bannockburn in 1314 and it became the Blarney Stone.

However in 1296, in conflict with the previous story, the Stone of Scone was taken by Edward I and taken to Westminster Abbey where it was fitted into a wooden chair known as St. Edward's chair in which all English monarchs were seated when being crowned. In spite of several attempts to return the Stone to Scotland, it still remains in England even though the theory is that it is not the original Stone of Scone, having been lost or hidden well. In the most recent history, in 1950, four Scottish students successfully hijacked the Stone and took it to Scotland where it remained for some time until the London police was involved and the Stone returned to Westminster Abbey. This did damage relations between the English and Scottish.

On November 15, 1996, the British government handed over the Stone of Scone to Scotland, where it currently resides at Edinburgh Castle with the provision that it be taken to Westminster Abbey when there is a coronation.

In spite of questions about the Stone's originality, it is said that it retains its ancient purpose of crowning Scottish monarchs, being that the current English monarchy also rules Scotland.

As for the Irish Stone of Destiny, it is supposedly a standing stone at the Inauguration Mound on the Hill of Tara (County Meath). The *Lia Fáil* served as the coronation stone for the High Kinds of Ireland up to Muirchertach mac Ercae in AD 500. Interestingly, the current stone on the hill was tested and found to be native to Ireland.

The *Lia Fáil* or Stone of Ireland, was apparently brought to the hill by the Tuatha Dé Danann, a semi-divine ancient race with magical arts and was supposed to roar when the rightful High King of Ireland set his foot on it. The stone also apparently had the power to give the king rejuvenation healing and a long reign. But it ceased to roar when Cúchulainn split it with his sword in anger when it did not roar for his pick as the High King, except for Conn of the Hundred Battles and Brian Boru.

The *Fianna Fáil*, Ireland's largest political party, took its name from the Stone and it is also used for the cap badge of the Irish Army as well as the opening lines of the Irish national anthem.

Stonehenge

Today Stonehenge, a prehistoric monument located in Wiltshire County, England, is in ruins as many of the stones have fallen or been removed by various people over the years for home construction or road repair. Many of the carvings on the stones and the surrounding stones, called "bluestones" are also damaged due to wear or from contact by the visitors, so it is currently protected by fencing around the site. In spite of the ruins, it is still a very impressive site surrounded by burial mounds.

Christopher Chippindale's *Stonehenge Complete* states that the meaning of Stonehenge comes from the Old English words "*stan*" meaning stone and either "*hencg*" meaning hinge (the stone lintels hinge on the upright stones) or "*hen(c)en*" meaning hang or gallows or instrument of torture. The term henge is a popular one with archaeologists, using it to describe earthworks consisting of a circular banked enclosure with an internal ditch, but Stonehenge is not considered a true henge site, as its bank is inside its ditch.

Stonehenge was constructed approximately 5,000 years ago. It is believed that the tools used to dig the ditch and the bank were made from the antlers of a deer, possibly wood and cattle shoulder blades and the dug up dirt was carried away in baskets. There are many theories as to how the stones forming the circles were transported, the most popular being that they were dragged by roller and sledge from the inland mountains to the waters and loaded onto boats from Wales to England, then hauled on land again and transported to the main site.

The giant sarsen (or main) stones weigh as much as 50 tons each and modern studies show that it could have taken at least 600 men to take transport stones from one place to another! Ropes and levers were used to set them up to hold the lintels along the top surfaces. There are also the bluestones, which were believed to come from the Prescelly Mountains located at the southwestern tip of Wales, 240 miles away and could weigh up to 40 tons each.

The mystery is who built Stonehenge. It was believed to have been started by the people of the late Neolithic period around 3000 B.C. and completed by a later generation. For those who believe in magic, a twelfth century writer named Geoffrey of Monmouth provides the story that it was Merlin who brought the stones, via his magic arts, to Salisbury Plain from Ireland at the high King Aurelius Ambrosius' request in order to honor men who were killed in a massacre by a treacherous Saxon leader. To this day, Stonehenge is a pilgrimage not only for awed tourists but for those who follow druidic or pagan beliefs.

Interestingly enough, even though Stonehenge is protected by fencing, with special permission from the English Heritage society, access is permitted during the summer and winter solstice and the spring and autumn equinox or by special booking.

T

Table-Tipping

Over time, many ways of communicating with spirits have evolved from rituals to the modern technology such as digital recorders for capturing voices and sounds. The Ouija board is one such popular method (although not a recommended one). Another method is "table turning" or "table tipping" which is not as widely used as the Ouija board.

Table turning began during the movement of Modern Spiritualism around 1852-1853. Because ordinary people did not have the means or access to professional mediums, the table turning was an answer to their interest in psychic phenomena as part of "home circles." Home circles were simply small groups of family and friends who got together to participate in these séances.

So, how does table turning work? Basically, it is a group of people sitting around a table, placing their hands on it and waiting for the table to make specific movements upon request. The table would vibrate and theoretically spell out words and sentences. Sometimes there would be wrappings or knockings. It became very fashionable in England and the English television show *Most Haunted* cast currently uses it as one of their tools for contacting the ghosts. There were several theories of what caused the movement of the tables. Dr. John Elliotson (1791-1868), an English physician, and his followers attributed the phenomena to mesmerism (also defined as animal magnetism or sexual charisma); Dr. James Braid, a Scottish surgeon (1795-1860) who was considered the father of modern hypnotism, and other followers suggested that it was the power of suggestion. However, it was Dr. Michael Faraday (1791-1867), a chemist and physicist, who invented an experiment that proved that the force at work tilting the table was an involuntary and unconscious muscle contraction of the fingers of the sitters. This was one of the reasons that led to the decline of the use of the tables to communicate with the spirits. However, this theory, according to the other believers, did not help explain why the tables lifted in the air and galloped about which would have been impossible to do with the involuntary muscular contractions of the fingers, so there is no universal agreement on what causes the table movements.

Conversely, a French teacher and educator by the name of Hippolyte Léon Denizard Rivail (1804-1869) who also went by the pseudonym Allan Kardec, the author of *The Spirits' Book, The Book on Mediums* and others, felt that an outside intelligence was involved. The basis for that reasoning was that he studied the phenomenon scientifically and many of the messages that came through contained information that was not known.

Another reason for the decline of the table turning was that it was often a long and tedious process to figure out the alphabet and other communication methods, whereas using the Ouija boards often brought quicker results. It also made it easy for people to fake the movement of the tables, which made it easy for it to be considered nothing more than a parlor game, although there have been stories that sometimes faking it caused genuine phenomena to occur!

In spite of fact there are a lot of documented cons against the use of table turning to communicate with spirits, there are still people who use it to this day such as the *Most Haunted* cast, mediums and others, it is merely another tool for experimenting with spirit communication, as with other tools, in the paranormal field.

Tutankhamen's Curse

One of the fathers of modern psychology, Dr. Carl Gustav Jung, created the term synchronicity in order to describe the relationship between meaningful coincidences. Ironically, Jung would allow the scarab beetle to play a key role in his description of his theory of synchronicity. The irony is that the scarab beetle was also used by the Ancient Egyptians as a symbol of rebirth, thus connecting Jung's theory of synchronicity to the Ancient Egyptians and a series of what could be considered either meaningful coincidences or what has also become known as Tutankhamen's curse.

It was on November 26th of 1922 that archaeologist Howard Carter would stand in front of his wealthy sponsor, the amateur Egyptologist Lord Carnarvon, as Carter broke through the tomb wall of KV62 in the Valley of the Kings that held the mummy and treasure of Ancient Egypt's only boy king. What those present were unaware of was the deadly fate that had been set in motion for some of them, as if riding out of the tomb on the back of a scarab beetle.

It would only be a few months after the opening of KV62 when Lord Carnarvon would be bitten by a mosquito on the cheek, a common carrier and mode for the transmission of disease. As a result, Lord Carnarvon would succumb to death's calling due to a secondary infection from the mosquito bite, which he cut while shaving.

When the media received word of the death of Lord Carnarvon, the stories about his death became greatly exaggerated. It was the newspapers that were the first to print what has now become known as the "actual" curse of the Pharaohs: *"Death shall come on swift wings to him who disturbs the peace of the King."*

Unfortunately, the written curse that was credited to having been inscribed on the wall of KV62 has never appeared there and was a complete fabrication of the newsprint of the era. Other media fabrications were the rumors that Lord Carnarvon's pet canary was killed by a cobra on the day the tomb was opened and that on the day of his passing, the Cairo city lights went black and his dog started to howl just prior to dropping dead without explanation.

While most of the dramatics seem to have been to sell newspapers and King Tut memorabilia, the facts seem to tell a very different tale. The truth is that while Lord Carnarvon's death still brings to mind tales of ancient curses, out of the 22 individuals that were present on that day in 1922 only six had actually died within 10 years and some of those individuals had been diagnosed with illnesses prior to 1922. As for Howard Carter, he actually lived to the ripe old age of 66 before he died of natural causes. But something happened that appeared not to rule out the possibility of the boy king's revenge entirely, in 1966 when the Egyptian Director of Antiquities was discussing the possibility of allowing the treasures found in the tomb to be sent to Paris for exhibition, that he was struck by a car and fatally injured.

U

Uisneach

Located west of Mullingar in Westmeath County, Ireland, Uisneach (pronounced *ooshnick*) is considered to be Ireland's "sacred navel" or *omphalos*, set square in the middle of Ireland. The ancient Kings of Ulster (North), Leinster (East), Munster (South) and Connaught (West) would get together at Uisneach for important meetings.

Its importance would seem to indicate it was a monumental location, but this was not the case. It is merely a 181 meters high limestone outcrop, but its advantage was that it was deep inland and thus provided needed sanctuary. Not much remains at Uisneach today except for a large catstone, some burial monuments and a fort. The catstone (so named as it seemed to resemble a cat) is said to mark the burial place of the mother goddess Eriu or Erin. According to Geoffrey of Monmouth's "History of the Kings of Britain," Stonehenge was transported to Britain from Uisneach.

Uisneach was traditionally favored for Beltane fires that could be seen all the way to Tara, who in turn had fires lit there and so on throughout the entire country of Ireland. Archaeologists have indeed discovered and documented that huge fires were burnt in the area since Neolithic times. Not only that, there were other rituals involving fire in which either animals were burnt as sacrifices or cattle driven through two fires to preserve them from future accidents. This tradition gave the meaning to the term "baptism by fire." St. Brigid, an Irish saint who is connected with fire, apparently took veil at Uisneach as well. Interestingly, there are two concentric beacon rings around the central Uisneach fire point that have been identified as the "fire eye" which has been discovered on other megalithic depictions such as the "Hill of Hag" at Loughcrew and others.

To this day, Ireland has maintained its division of counties through the site of Uisneach, and druids, pilgrims and pagans continued to visit there to celebrate rituals. One of the co-authors has visited Uisneach Hill when it was private property in 2002, thanks to one of her friends who knew the owner and understood at that time it would be open to the public shortly. She has not seen any indication if that has actually happened or not.

Unidentified Submersible Objects

While UFO sightings seem to be embedded in many forms of human history and documented records, there is another phenomenon that remains less known, but equally documented. The phenomenon is often commonly referred to by the acronym, USO, which stands for "Unidentified Submersible Objects." One of the most famous historical sightings took place back in 1492 during Christopher Columbus' voyage to discover America.

If the truth be known, USOs were actually just as widely reported as UFOs prior to the famed Kenneth Arnold sighting. One such case was reported by a Royal Australian Air Force officer by the name of William Brennan. Lieutenant Brennan was assigned to patrol the Bass Strait south of Melbourne Australia to look for Japanese submarines or German U-boats. The local fisherman had reported seeing strange lights on the ocean at night just after the Japanese had attacked Darwin on February 19, 1942.

While flying his patrol over Tasmania at around 6:00p.m., Lt. Brennan spotted an object that he described as being 50 feet in diameter and about 150 feet in length. Lt. Brennen also reported seeing what looked like a dome on top of the craft and he noted that the craft paced his aircraft for several minutes until it suddenly made an abrupt dive, not crash, into the ocean. He also reported seeing what appeared to him to be four fins on the craft's underside as it made its descent into the water.

Not just occurring abroad, one sighting in January of 1956 was witnessed by well over two dozen reputable individuals just off the coast of Redondo Beach in California. It involved both police and security personnel who reported seeing a large glowing object skimming over the top of the water and then suddenly diving below the waves. Once it was below the waves, the witnesses all reported still being able to see the glow of the object moving for some time. Concerned, authorities sent divers to the scene to investigate. When they arrived at the site, the object was nowhere to be found.

There have been several explanations for this particular phenomenon, but only two primary hypotheses. The first is that they are the result of natural phenomenon, such as, phosphorescent jellyfish and other phosphorescent sea life swimming in large schools being observed by witnesses standing on shore. These witnesses see them at a distance with the curvature of the earth creating the illusion that they are in flight as they swim farther away and dive into the water as they get closer, when in reality they are simply a line of sight mirage.

The second primary hypothesis is one that was first presented by anthropologist, Dr. Roger Wescott, back in 1969. His hypothesis, while not well accepted by his colleagues, stated that at some point in earth's ancient history aliens visited this planet and found that humans were not advanced enough to accept their help and that it would take thousands of years to ever bring us up to their advanced level of thinking. So they decided to stay on earth by building bases under the water and taking with them a few humans to train and re-introduce at set intervals.

V

Valentino's Ghost

One of the most famous silent movie stars was Rudolph Valentino, who over a nine-year period, made movies such as *The Sheik*, *The Son of the Sheik*, *Monsieur Beaucaire* and *The Four Horsemen of the Apocalypse*. He developed very rapidly a following of women from all over the world to the point where he had to hire security guards, trained dogs and other protection of himself and his property.

Rudolph Valentino was the product of an Italian middle-class upbringing who immigrated to New York where he started working as a dancer. Because of his visible sensuality, he rose quickly to fame and fortune in the movies, becoming one of the first "heart-throbs" of the movies. But he developed a perforated ulcer for which he underwent surgery and developed peritonitis, dying at the age of 31.

He was such a popular idol that his death caused mass hysteria and even suicides among his following. It was shortly thereafter that sightings of ghosts began to surface.

His main residence which was called Falcon's Lair, was a huge house on a hilltop overlooking Beverly Hills on eight acres of land, including stables, garages and servant housing. A stable worker, coming to work one day, saw the apparition of Valentino grooming a favorite horse and fled in terror, never to return. A fellow actor reported seeing Valentino's ghost wandering the halls and rooms and an actress who tried to spend the night there was chased out by it. Over the years, passersby have seen Valentino's phantom staring out of the windows.

His ghost has also been reported in his beach house in Oxnard and an inn in Santa Maria as well in the wardrobe department of Paramount Studios, where he just appears and doesn't bother anyone. In life, he was a flashy dresser.

It also has been reported that people visiting the pet cemetery, where Kabar, Valentino's beloved Great Dane, is buried, have seen the big pup's apparition play among the grave markers!

Valley of the Moon

The Valley of the Moon region was made famous by Jack London, one of the most prolific and highly paid writers of his time, over one hundred years ago and is the site of many well-known hauntings, particularly the Sonoma and Glen Ellen areas. Jack London moved to the Valley of the Moon area near Glen Ellen at the beginning of the 20th century as he disliked the city life. He bought 1,200 acres and constructed many buildings where he wrote many of his famous stories. The main building was a renovated 1860's ranch house that Jack and his wife Charmian lived in during his final years of his life. He also built Wolf House, but it burned in a fire in 1913.

Jack London died on November 22, 1916 at the age of 40 due to the excesses of his heavy drinking and other illnesses never properly diagnosed. A few months after he died, Charmain London reported in her memoir that she saw his ghost in the field in front of the ranch house "stepping blithely, whistling comradely to an unmistakable friend shadowing his heel – Peggy the Beloved, our small canine Irish saint." In the ranch house itself, people, including his relatives, reported hearing footsteps and doors slamming open and shut on its own.

Wolf House was to be Jack London's showplace, being carved from volcanic rock and consisting of rooms more than 50 feet long, with redwood timbers, floors and rafters. Jack and his wife meant to move in there upon its completion, but before they could, it was destroyed by a fire, the cause unknown. Only the walls and redwood timbers remained standing and Jack wanted to rebuild it but never did. Auditory and visual phenomena have been reported in the Wolf House, including partial apparitions, the sound of metal hammers striking rock and heavy boots stepping about, as though the workers were still hard at work.

Interestingly, Jack London's mother was a devout Spiritualist who conducted séances at their home for a living even though Jack London really was not very involved in the occult, although some of his writings do mention it.

Today 800 acres of Jack London's property, including the ranch house and Wolf House are open to hikers, equestrians and tourists. Other locations in the Valley of the Moon such as Valley of the Moon Saloon, Mission San Francisco Solano, General Vallejo's home, Sebastiani Vineyards and Winery and the Blue Wing Inn are other places well worth a visit to investigate alleged hauntings.

W

Winchester Mystery House

How would you like to play hide and seek in a house with 160 rooms, 47 fireplaces, 10,000 window panes, 17 chimneys, two basements and three working elevators? And to make matters worse, there are doors and stairways that go nowhere, making the game of hide and seek impossible and confusing. Who would want to play the game, let alone live there?

Yet it was Sarah Winchester who built such a home to live and "play" in nearly total isolation (with the exception of her servants, workmen and her niece who was her constant companion which began as an 8-room farmhouse in San Jose, California. Over the next 38 years from 1884 to 1922, it grew, with the help of workmen 24 hour a day, 365 days a year, to a mansion now known as the Winchester Mystery House (525 South Winchester Blvd., San Jose, CA 95128).

The Winchester Mystery House is famous for its size and lack of any master building plan. It was originally seven stories on 162 acres and it is estimated that over 600 rooms were built and then torn down to the current remaining four stories and 160 rooms today on 4.5 acres. Why build such a crazy house? According to legend, Sarah Winchester went to see a psychic medium in Boston to seek some kind of consolation after the deaths of her daughter Annie in 1866 and her husband William Wirt Winchester. The medium apparently told Sarah Winchester that she was haunted by vengeful ghosts who were killed by guns made by the Winchester Repeating Arms Company. There are several variations of this medium's reading, but the end result was that Sarah Winchester moved out West to build a house in order to either appease or confuse the spirits and to ensure her "immortality."

Building the house 24 hours a day, for 365 days a year for 38 years? How could she afford it? Because Sarah Winchester received nearly 50% ownership of the Winchester Repeating Arms Company upon her husband's death to the tune of $20 million, it ensured that she received an income of $1,000 per day which was not taxable until 1913 (today that amount would be roughly $21,000 per day). The estimated total cost was $5.5 million (today it would be almost $70 million!). When Sarah Winchester died on September 5, 1922, workmen stopped hammering the nails halfway in and this is visible today.

The house had modern conveniences that were rare for such times such as modern indoor toilets and plumbing, push-button gas lights, a hot shower from indoor plumbing and even three elevators! Additionally, there were designs throughout the house reflecting Sarah Winchester's beliefs such as number 13 and spider web motifs. Upon Sarah Winchester's death, her will was in 13 parts and signed 13 times. One of the most important features of the house was a bell tower, in which the bell was rung at midnight to summon the spirits and again at 2 AM to signal the spirits to leave.

More details about the Winchester Mystery House can be found on several websites throughout the internet. With such a unique history, it is no wonder that the mansion is allegedly haunted. The reports of hauntings have included:

- Footsteps and mysterious voices
- Cold spots
- Strange lights – red lights have been reported in the bedroom where Sarah Winchester died
- Sarah Winchester's apparition

- Apparitions of servants and workmen, including a workman with a mustache in overalls pushing a wheelbarrow

    Today, the Winchester Mystery House is a California Historical Landmark and is registered with the National Park Service as "a large, odd dwelling with an unknown number of rooms," a sad tribute to a lonely, melancholic, eccentric and tiny 4'10" woman, who used to be the belle of the ball in her hometown with musical skills, fluency in several languages and charm until the deaths of her daughter and husband. Whether it is actually haunted or not, the Winchester Mystery House is a very intriguing site well worth a visit. Several tours are available, including flashlight tours at night around Halloween and Friday the 13th.

X, Y & Z

Yeti

A creature known to millions as a symbol of both Mt. Everest and the Himalayas, is the mysterious and elusive Yeti. A bipedal hairy ape-like beast that has been known to the local Sherpas for centuries and some accounts by Alexander the Great even claim that the beast exists.

The Yeti has become a part of Western pop culture just prior to the beginning of the 20th century and its first notations in the logs of B.H. Hodgson in 1832, who mentioned that his native guides had seen a tall, dark and hairy creature running away on two legs. Hodgson noted that he did not actually witness the creature and that he suspected that what his guides had actually saw was nothing more than an orangutan.

It was L.A. Wadell who was one of the first Westerners to take the local reports of the Yeti seriously enough to take the time to formally interview local witnesses who had seen both the creature and its footprints back in 1889. After talking with many of the local witnesses, Wadell reached the final conclusion that all the sightings of bipedal hair animals, were nothing more that bears in an upright aggressive bipedal posturing.

Wadell's conclusion would not be enough to silence the talk of the Yeti, because in 1921, a British Expedition led by Colonel C.K. Howard-Bury would attempt to climb the northern face of Mt. Everest. During that attempt, the team spotted, not one, but several hairy bipedal creatures moving above them at about 17,000 feet in the snow. When the team reached that altitude, they discovered several large tracks in the snow that were too large to be human. Col. Howard-Bury claimed that the footprints were nothing more than those of an over sized grey wolf, but the Sherpas immediately identified them as those of a Yeti.

Sightings and reports continued, but it was Eric Shipton who was the first westerner to bring full media attention to the Yeti with his famous photographs of footprints taken in Nepal in 1951. The photos have been subject to great debate because of the medium that the footprints were made in. The problem is that the tracks were left in snow which melts causing tracks to become deformed. This has left many to argue that the tracks are nothing more than those of normal animals that have been deformed by melting snow, while others claim they are proof of the existence of the Yeti.

One thing is clear, and that is whether or not there is really a Yeti, one indisputable fact exists about it, and that is that it has become a permanent part of the regional culture and international pop culture. The evidence has been made clear in everything from the airline named after the creature that serves the isolated population of Nepal or the annual children's Christmas animated film featuring the *Abominable Snowman*, a western nickname for the Yeti.